Catherine Mede

A MODERN DAY RETELLNG

CAROL'S CHRISTMAS

Carol's Christmas
Copyright © (2025) by Catherine Mede

Publisher: Flying Kiwi Press
Cover Design: Copyright (2025) © K Parker

Breast cancer is the biggest killer of women in New Zealand. Check your breasts often.

Disclaimer: The characters and events in this book are the creation of the author, and resemblance to persons, whether living or dead, is strictly coincidental. Businesses, towns and places are used as settings and have no relation to any event or actually happening outside the authors' imagination.

ISBN 978-1-0670901-1-1 Amazon
ISBN 978-1-0607901-2-8 paperback
ISBN 978-1-0607901-3-5 Epub
ISBN 978-1-0607901-4-2 PDF

Dedication

To Leanne and Trudi,
and all of the other heroine's out there who have
fought and won.

Christmas Past

"I told you these were shadows of the things that have been."
Said the Ghost. "That they are what they are, do not blame me."

A Christmas Carol
Charles Dickens

Chapter One

Christmas Eve

Some people call me selfish and greedy. I prefer driven and focused.

The most important thing to me is my business.

My foot tapped excitedly against the side of my desk as I listened to the other person on my cell phone.

"Yes...aha...yes..." I agreed, a I could feel the grin pulling on my cheeks and a bubbly feeling in my chest.

Rolling my eyes, I pull a face at Iona Crossman, who was sitting opposite me. I picked up a pencil and placed it at the top of my writing pad. I'd stopped taking notes long ago. My scrawl across the page only had three words: 'Get more product!' which I directed Iona to look at. She nodded and smiled.

"Yes, I agree. I'll see what I can do." I listened to the other person, but really it was a blur of words. "Aha, yes, okay, will call you later. Bye."

I pressed 'end call' and did a happy dance.

"Good news?" Iona asked, pushing her brunette hair off her face.

I looked at her like she'd grown another head. "Yes, Amanda from Corporate Facilities. They want more, and they want it now." What had started as a small one-person operation making carryall's, had turned into a lucrative business making satchels and bags with company logos embroidered on them.

Iona sighed. "Doesn't everyone? Did you tell them it's Christmas and that will not happen?"

Carol's Christmas

I bit my bottom lip. I had said nothing of the kind. I didn't want to lose this contract.

"Carol!" Iona's voice whined. "Come on, chick, it's Christmas. Your staff need a break."

"They can work until five. It's only Christmas Eve."

"Carol, it's Christmas *Eve*," she emphasised. "They finish up at twelve thirty and no later. Your staff have worked hard for you all year. They deserve this break."

"But I need to get this order out." Now my voice sounded whiney, and I hated it. I hated when I had to argue with my bestie about my company.

Iona planted her hands firmly on my desk, leaning towards me. "No. Your staff need this two-week holiday."

I wanted to slam my fists down, but I resisted the urge. It didn't look good when the head of the company had a tantrum. Instead, I looked her in the eye. She remained firm, not cowering to my withering look. I sighed.

"Fine. Out." I pointed to the door.

Iona side-eyed me and nodded as she left the office.

I groaned as I bent over and banged my head on the desk. I had great staff, yes, but what happened to ethics and responsibility and making it work? It was my business, and I wanted it to be a success. Entrepreneur of the Year wasn't enough, a multi-million-dollar business wasn't enough. I needed to show the world that I was something, could make something of myself and make money at it.

I glanced at my watch. It was ten thirty Christmas Eve. I might get some of my staff to work between Christmas and New Year. But would it be enough?

I stood and brushed the creases out of my skirt and blouse and walked down into the workroom.

"Anyone keen to work between Christmas and New Year?" I shouted over the noise. The machines went silent, and a few people muttered, passing on the request.

"Do we get double time?" a voice shouted.

"Ah, no," I said.

"Time in lieu?"

I couldn't see who called out.

"Nope," I replied.

The chorus of no's was drowned out by the sound of the machines as they whirred back into motion.

No one wanted to work?

How dare they.

I stormed back into my office, trying to keep the fire in my chest at bay. After all I'd done for these people. I'd given them jobs, kept the business open, barely, through Covid and re-employed all of my team. I paid them well, maybe too well. Their rejection burned me to the core, and I wondered where I'd gone wrong. Maybe I paid them too much money? Gave them too many days off. They got the two weeks over Christmas and New Year. They had another week or two of holidays, depending on how long they'd been with the company.

I'd built Laroc Originals from the ground up, employed the best staff. I gave them the occasional perks, but they gave very little back in return.

Covid had been hard. I'd had the government subsidy to keep things going, and I'd worked by myself in the workshop, even produced some products that could be useful to hospital staff so that I had some income coming in. I paid my staff their wages, even though it ate into the business savings. When the lockdowns eased, my staff came back, but they had been rather...lethargic wasn't the right word. They hadn't been as keen to work as they had before. And now, having to pay back the subsidy was another cost that I had to cope with. This latest offer, to purchase a phenomenal amount of my product, was just the ticket I needed for the business to recover. But they wanted it by the start of

Carol's Christmas

February, and there was no way I could get it to them unless the company worked through Christmas.

Why didn't my staff have the same drive as I did? I put my head down and worked through the business accounting books until I heard laughing out in the workshop. Glancing at my watch, I noticed it was twelve thirty. I sighed as I got up from my desk. I placed a hand on the door handle, forced a smile, and opened the door.

I walked out into the workshop, laughing and briefly chatting with the staff as they were cleaning up from the shared lunch that we traditionally had on Christmas Eve, before they left the workshop. Iona and I stood alone on the clean shop floor, dust motes from its recent sweep still hovering in the air. The machines cleaned and tidied and silent. All ready to start again after New Year's.

Iona clapped me on the back. "Well done, boss. You handled that well."

"Thanks," I replied, my voice flat. My shoulders felt heavy as I stood looking at her. I didn't feel like celebrating, I had planning to do.

"I'll lock up," I told Iona. "Have a good Christmas." I hugged her before heading back to my office to continue working.

I might have to make the call and tell the customer that they wouldn't get the order until after February. But it wasn't something I was comfortable doing. What if they removed the order? That wouldn't work for me.

I went out into the factory and sat at a machine, starting it up, before heading over and getting the material ready to create more of what I needed.

Chapter Two

Christmas Day

"Morning, Mum!" Emma jumped on my bed, waking me with a start. "Merry Christmas!"

I pulled my daughter into a hug. "Morning, Ems, Merry Christmas." I cuddled her, tucking her under the blankets as I did so, closing my eyes again. Slowly my mind drifted off, back to darkness, and sleep...

"Come on, Mum." I jerked awake at the sound of Em's voice as she bounced out of my bed.

I sighed. "What time is it?" I forgot my daughter wasn't so little anymore.

"Eight...in the morning," she said.

I groaned. I'd been awake until about three this morning, working out how to get the factory more productive in order to fulfil the order by February. Five hours wasn't nearly enough sleep.

"You open the presents without me," I said, pulling the blankets over my head and imagining the pouty look on Em's face. She was sixteen, tall and lanky, and full of energy that made me jealous. I used to love when she was little and would snuggle with me in bed until she fell asleep. However, she wasn't five anymore. But I didn't dwell on it for too long, because I drifted back to sleep.

I awoke with a start and looked at the clock beside her bed—10:13 a.m. I yawned and stretched as I listened to the quiet house. I could vaguely hear Christmas carols being played but couldn't make out which song it was. That would be Ems, trying to inject the Christmas spirit into the house. I hadn't bothered with decorations or a tree, but Ems had pulled some out and put tinsel along the hearth and around the firebox. She'd put a pot plant on the top of the firebox and placed some baubles on its leaves, making them dip low, almost touching the cold fire plate. It was the middle of summer here. Not that I wanted a winter Christmas, I didn't do cold.

Christmas was just another day for me. I'd never enjoyed celebrating it before I'd had Ems and had suffered through the childhood need for Christmas, but as Em's got older, and after Noah left, I felt even less inclined to celebrate. That hadn't stopped her from trying to kick-start me into enjoying the season.

Christmas, when I was a kid, was a sombre affair. We were lucky if we got a stocking with an orange in it. Mostly we got second-hand clothes, maybe a book. And my parents did nothing but argue and bicker about unnecessary spending of money.

Now that Ems was sixteen, it was easier to just let things go. The smell of bacon and coffee wafted through the house and my stomach gurgled, reminding me it was well past breakfast time.

This was our second Christmas without Noah. The first one had been really hard. I think I spent most of the day crying once Noah had picked Ems up. I didn't know what to do with myself. Iona had her family, Mum was up north, and Christmas kind of snuck up on me. The same sense of sadness pulled at my heart as I tied my bathrobe around me and put my feet into my battered old slippers and scuffed my way down towards the kitchen.

"Morning again," Ems said, her eyebrows drawn low over her eyes. She wasn't happy. Coffee was steaming in a cup which she gave to me as I wandered into the kitchen.

"Morning, sweetie." I kissed my daughter on the cheek, but she continued making pancakes as if I wasn't there.

"We'll have breakfast first, then sort out presents," she said, sounding efficient and taking on the parental role.

"Sounds good. Smells good," I said, as I looked over her shoulder at the pot with scrambled eggs in it.

"Yes, great Christmas fare," Ems grumbled.

I set the table and sat down with my coffee. Plates of pancakes, bacon, scrambled eggs, and maple syrup were set down and we tucked in. Neither of us talked while we ate. I read through the news on my phone, as I did every morning, while Ems kept throwing glances my way. Occasionally, I would catch her glares over the top of my phone, but I ignored it. I was tired and grumpy and didn't want to deal with teenage angst on my one day off work.

Once we'd finished eating, Ems ushered me into the lounge, where some small packages sat beside the pot plant on the fireplace. She was suddenly more animated, and she handed me three boxes. Carefully wrapped and tied with a ribbon and bow. I opened each box and delighted in my daughter's thoughtfulness. A beautiful porcelain figurine of a mother and daughter, a lovely necklace of our birth stones, an aquamarine, and a ruby. The last one was a leather satchel I could use for work. She'd obviously overhead me talking about needing something bigger than a handbag to take documents to and from work.

"Thank you, Ems, they're beautiful."

"I'm pleased you liked them." Ems ducked her head, hiding her blush and pride at my praise. Her eyes were glowing when she looked back up at me. She was a different person when we weren't arguing or sniping at each other. Her hands were fidgeting in her lap.

"Now open yours." I suggested.

An envelope sat beside the pot. Ems picked it up and quickly tore into the card. A gift card slipped out for one hundred dollars at Pandoras. Ems read through the card, turned it over, and picked up the gift card.

"Gee, thanks, Mum." She hugged me, and I thought I saw tears in her eyes. She buried her head in my shoulder, but I could feel her taking deep breaths. I'd taken a long time to think about what to get Ems, but I couldn't think of anything. And I'd bought her a Pandora bracelet last Christmas, so I thought she could get herself another charm or two.

"Is that it?" Ems asked.

I looked around the lounge. There were no other presents visible.

"Yes, that's it."

"You really put a lot of thought into my Christmas present, didn't you?" she said, not hiding the bitterness in her voice.

I sat back, my face warming up as if she'd slapped me.

"I'm busy, Ems, I can't get out much to have a look around, you know that."

"You're busy?" She huffed. "I found time between being at school, studying and working at the supermarket, to find you thoughtful gifts. Check your priorities, Mum."

"Ouch, that's hurtful, Ems. You know I care about you."

"Do you? All I know is that you drove Dad away, and you don't really care about me. You didn't even try to find out what I might have liked."

I tried not to show the shock that I felt, the burning sensation in my gut at her words. "What do you mean? I work hard to make sure you have a roof over your head."

"Yeah, thanks, Mum. When was the last time we went out for coffee or a girls' shopping trip?"

"I don't have time for that."

"I know, Mum, because business is more important than me."

I roll my eyes at her exaggerated tone. "That's not true. We've done lots of things together."

"Really? When was the last time we went to the movies?"

I thought back over the past year. I couldn't remember when I'd last spent some time with her. She was right. It had been a while.

"I'm sorry, honey. I promise, after this order, we'll go out and spend some time together."

Ems sighed, tears forming in her eyes again. "You say that every time. And every time it doesn't happen. Mum, I love you, but you really are a shit parent."

"Don't use that language, young lady."

"I'm nearly seventeen. I think I'm old enough to have an opinion of my own."

I was completely dumbfounded. When had my baby girl gotten so big and adult? How had she grown up and I not notice?

I hung my head. "I'm sorry, I didn't realise how bad things have been."

"Mum, they were bad before Dad left. Why do you think he left?"

"Because he didn't love me anymore."

"Wrong. He left because you cared more about your stupid business than you did about him. You don't care about me, but I stuck around to be there for you, but you know what, I'm really regretting that decision." She stomped out of the room, muttering down the hallway as she went.

I sat back on the couch and looked at the lovely, thoughtful presents that Ems had given me. Things that she knew I liked or wanted. Careful thought and consideration had gone into those things. But I'd been too busy, had rushed out to the local Pandora supplier and bought a voucher. Not a lot of thought or consideration was required.

Ems was right, I was a shit parent.

Chapter Three

The doorbell rang, and Ems pounded down the hallway to answer it. Noah's voice drifted into my office, and I came out, smiling. My core ached with loneliness because I still loved him. I couldn't stop that emotion from happening, and every time I heard his voice, my heart thrilled, and my blood sang.

"Hey," I said, leaning on the doorframe. I'd always admired Noah for his charm and good looks. I'd been so thrilled when he'd asked me out on a date when we were still teenagers. He was nineteen and I was seventeen, having a gap year before university. We'd immediately hit it off, and we'd become each other's lives...until we weren't.

"Hey, yourself. How's things?" he asked, his smile making his eyes glisten. One hand was in his pocket, and the other one was swinging his car keys around and catching them. Everything about him was so casual and relaxed, the complete opposite of me.

"Don't go there, Dad," Ems grumbled, appearing out of nowhere.

"Hey, kiddo, go easy on your mum."

"She's already given me my pedigree today," I said.

Noah rolled his eyes and looked at Ems.

"She deserved it, okay?" she replied.

"Yeah, I did. Anyway, things are great. A new order just came through, so gearing up to get that done. They need it by February," I replied, pleased with myself. My mouth felt dry, and I licked my lips to moisten them.

"Oh, so things are going well in the business, then."

I ignored the sarcasm I heard in his voice. I wouldn't listen to another lecture from him.

"Yeah, going well."

"Okay, great." He turned to Emma. "How about you put your stuff in the car? I'll be there shortly." Ems picked up her bag and opened the door, without saying goodbye to me. A familiar ache resonated in my heart, but I smiled through the pain, brushing it off, trying to keep my focus on Noah.

"Oi, Ems, come and say goodbye to your mum," he called out to her, and I heard faintly from the driveway Ems saying goodbye. I closed my eyes and swallowed, trying to push the lump back down my throat.

"Carol." Noah reached out and touched my arm. The warmth stirred something within me, and I thought my knees would give out. Even though we weren't together anymore, I still wanted him, and he could make me have all the feels. To me, Noah was as handsome as the day I first met him. His hair was salt and pepper now, compared to the dark brown of his youth. His eyes were a beautiful bronze colour that sparkled and lit up whenever he saw me. I loved how I fitted nicely under his arms when he cuddled me.

"Hmm," I responded. I was hoping he'd say something nice.

"You're going to lose Ems if you're not careful. You don't want two of us walking out on you."

I straightened up and stared at him. "She's just a kid."

"She's nearly seventeen, old enough to make up her own mind. I know I'm not supposed to have her until tomorrow, but she rang me up in tears. She's devastated, Carol. You need to pull your head in and realise that you have a life outside of the business."

And here was the lecture. I took a step back and crossed my arms. "She knows that I'm busy."

"She also needs her mum to be there and listen to her."

"I am here for her."

"Really? Where were you when she rang me?"

Carol's Christmas

I opened my mouth, but Noah beat me to it. "In your office. Our little girl is growing up, and you're missing it. You're too focused on money and success. Don't lose her too."

He stepped closer, hugged me, and then left.

The noise of the door shutting echoed through the silent house.

Here I was, standing in a large modern three-bedroom place I bought with my money and all on my own.

On Christmas Day.

I twirled my engagement and wedding bands on my finger. I hadn't taken them off yet, I couldn't. I kept clinging to the fact that we were separated, not divorced. It was a link with Noah, and I didn't want to lose that too. But the longer Noah stayed away, the more I realised that we probably weren't going to get back together.

I could sit and worry about it or focus on the business at hand. Getting that order completed.

I went back into my office and picked up the phone. "Iona, Merry Christmas," I said when my best friend answered.

"Ems is at her dads, isn't she?" Iona said.

I sighed and sunk into my office chair. "Yip, just came and got her."

"I told you that you needed to think about what you were getting her. Money isn't the answer. She wants her mum."

"Not you too. I just had that lecture from Noah."

"And don't get me started on how you lost the best thing that ever happened to you."

"Yeah, yeah, I get it. No lectures, please."

"What are you going to do about it?" Iona asked.

My laugh was bitter. "There isn't much I can do. Ems is now with Noah for the next two weeks, and I have a large order that needs to be completed by February."

"You're not starting on that again, are you?"

"Iona, I need to get this order out. It's an important client."

"And you have nearly three weeks once we return to get it done."

"That isn't enough time. I'm going into the factory this afternoon."

"You can't do it by yourself."

"I've done it before. I'm going to have to."

"Don't expect me to come in. I have my family, and they're important to me, and if you knew better, you would spend time with Noah and Ems."

"You're no bloody help then, are you?" I said, trying to sound like I was joking, but my friend's rejection cut deep. I'd hoped that she would come and help, but she had her own responsibilities.

"I'll catch you later. Merry Christmas," I said, then hung up the phone and dropped my head in my hands. My heart ached to the core with longing. I wanted my family back. It was Christmas Day, and I had no one to spend it with.

Admittedly, I'd planned nothing for Christmas dinner.

Again.

I thought about contacting Noah and spending time with him and Ems, but it hurt too much. I couldn't handle looking at him, knowing that we were no longer a couple, and having that pain reverberating around my body. He'd made it clear that while I had the business, he wasn't interested in being my husband because I wouldn't spend time with him.

And it was true, but he didn't realise just how important this business was to me. My family hadn't been rich. They'd really struggled to make ends meet, and I'd sworn that I wouldn't let that happen to me or my family. But I'd lost a few friends along the way; Iona was my only friend now. I'd grown this company with my bare hands, making products, buying the machines, slowly building up my workforce as the business took off. I'd created jobs, helped people out, given people a chance that no one had given me.

Me? Selfish? Would a selfish person work her butt off to give people a chance to better themselves?

The house was empty without Ems. I could hear the clock in the kitchen ticking down the seconds of the day. I sat in silence for a good minute, contemplating the quietness and how I missed the hustle and bustle that the house used to have. Now it was an empty, silent shell.

I sighed. Now was as good a time as any to ring Mum.

"Hello, darling. Merry Christmas."

"Merry Christmas, Mum," I said. "How are things?"

There was a lot of background noise and bursts of laughter. "Great, Aunt Anthea invited around some orphans, so we're having a blast," she yelled at me over the phone.

"Orphans?" I didn't understand what she meant.

"Those without parents or children. Anthea calls them her Christmas orphans."

"Sounds like you're having fun." A burning sensation formed in the pit of my stomach.

"We're having a ball. What about you? Where's Emma?"

"Ems is with her dad. I'm home alone," I said, staring around my empty lounge, kitchen, and dining area.

"Why aren't you with them?"

"I've got work to do."

"On Christmas Day?"

"Yeah, Mum, I do."

"Well, sounds like you need to lighten up."

"Yeah, thanks, Mum, I gotta go," I said, before hanging up. Between Iona, Noah, Mum and Ems, I didn't need any more guilt trips.

I closed my eyes and took a deep breath. I needed to get some work done. And I needed to do that now and shift my focus to getting started so that I had enough product to fulfil the order.

Chapter Four

January

For the two weeks between Christmas and the restarting of work in the New Year, I went into the factory and spent every day on the machines, getting the carryalls made. I mass-produced in sections to make the job easier and could work through each section methodically. By the time the staff returned to work in the New Year, I had most of the order sorted. It gave me three weeks to get the rest completed, and there was the occasional late night to make sure that they got it all done.

By the first of February, the order was done and shipped out. Everyone was exhausted.

"Don't put your staff under that sort of pressure again," Iona warned. She plopped down in the chair opposite my desk. She was the only person I allowed to talk to me like that.

"I didn't put them under any pressure as I did most of the work," I replied, sitting down in my leather seat behind my desk. Iona picked up her glass of wine. It was six on a Thursday evening, and we were celebrating getting the order out.

"Taking an order like that between Christmas and New Year was idiotic. Did you spend any time with Ems?"

I put my head down, the heat crawling up my cheeks. "She spent all her holidays with Noah. She only came home Sunday night."

"And what did you do when she got home?"

I looked up, confused. "Nothing, why?"

"You could've taken her out for a meal, or a movie."

"I was—"

"Too busy," Iona replied at the same time as I did. "Same old story. You better get in touch with your daughter before it's too late. She loves you, but she doesn't think you love her."

"How do you know that?"

"She talks to me."

"She doesn't—"

"Talk to you," Iona said at the same time. "And you know why. You're never there for her."

"Ouch." I tried to make out that I was joking, but pain flared in my chest. A deep hollow ache that seemed to be a constant companion lately.

"I'll try to be there for her this week. I have time now. The job is done."

"Parenting isn't on a week-by-week basis," Iona said. She took a sip of wine.

I nodded. "I know. I'll take her out to the movies tonight."

"It's a school night." Iona stated.

"For goodness' sake, Iona! Damned if I do and damned if I don't!" I let my frustration bubble up inside me. I knew I was safe to let it loose on her. She'd been with me through thick and thin and knew that I would settle down quickly enough.

"Take her out for tea or something."

I glanced at my watch. "She's probably already cooked dinner."

"Then what are you doing sitting here?" She raised her eyebrows as she emptied her wineglass. Mine was still full. I sat back in my chair and waved my hand at her. "And what are you doing here? Go home," I said.

Iona got up and walked to the door.

"Do something nice for Ems. Let her know you care."

"I will," I waved her out the door and sat at my desk, staring at my glass of wine. Iona was right, I should do something nice for

Ems. I tipped the wine into my pot plant and, grabbing my new satchel, locked the office and the workshop and headed home.

"Hey, Ems," I said as I walked in the door. I put my satchel in the office and headed into the kitchen. Ems was out of her uniform and in some casual clothes. The rice cooker was sitting on the bench, the light on warm as she stirred food around the wok.

"Hey, Mum, have a good day?"

"Yeah, got that order shipped today. Want to go out for dessert to celebrate?" Em's head jerked up from the stove.

"Yeah, sounds good." Her face lit up with a smile, and my heart lifted. I gave her a kiss on her cheek and set the table. We sat and talked while we ate tea, Ems telling me about her day, what had happened in her art class, and a joke she'd heard. I laughed as it was a terrible dad joke. It was nice to spend time with her. I really enjoyed it, and we had a few laughs.

We rushed through the dishes, then, passing her the keys, she drove us to a local restaurant.

"We're closing soon," they said as we rushed in.

"We're only after dessert and a coffee," I said.

The maitre'd bowed and showed us to a table. We glanced over the dessert menu and made our decisions. I had a chocolate sundae, while Ems chose a Death by Chocolate cheesecake and two hot chocolates.

The conversation dried up pretty quickly, and we sat in an awkward silence as we waited for the dessert and drinks. It wasn't too bad; we were together, and that was the main thing.

"How were the holidays with your dad?" I asked, trying to think of something to talk about.

"It was good. I got to meet Dad's new girlfriend," she said.

My heart lurched and sank in my chest. I tried to keep the smile on my face as we talked, but her words had stunned me and added to that painful hollowness that I was feeling. I didn't think that

Noah would move on. Well, maybe not that quickly. I thought that perhaps we still had a chance, but obviously we don't.

"That's nice. What's she like?" I asked, the smile making my cheeks sore.

"She's nice, a little flaky, but nice."

The fact Ems thought she was flaky gave my heart a wee lift, but not enough. I couldn't get past Noah having someone else in his life. We'd been together since school, and although he'd left just a year ago, I didn't think he would get over me that quickly.

Dessert arrived, and I shovelled the food into my mouth, giving myself an ice cream headache, but I just wanted to get out of that restaurant. I wanted to go home, crawl into our...no...my bed, and cry, swear, yell, call him ugly names, everything to make the pain in my heart ease, but I knew it wouldn't.

The pain was still as fresh as the day he walked out the door.

I'd known for a while that he wasn't happy. It was late spring because I remember it was a bitter day. I was in my home office till midnight. The heat pump was churning away, heating the house since it was too warm to have a fire, but too cold to not have something heating the house. Ems was in bed. I thought Noah was asleep, too, which is why I'd sneaked out of our room and come down here.

"What are you doing?" he'd asked, scaring the life out of me. I clutched my chest.

"Don't do that to me," I said as he came into the room, blinking at the brightness of the light.

"Come back to bed."

"I will. Just need to get caught up on my paperwork."

"Can't that wait until the morning?"

"No, I need to get it done now. I have other work that needs doing in the morning."

"This is the fifth time you've sneaked out of bed in the last two weeks."

"I'm sorry. I thought you were asleep."

"I was wondering what you were doing. I thought you were having an online affair or something."

"Pfft!" I attempted to brush off his concerns, but the look on his face persisted. "I'm too busy to have an affair."

"I'm serious. Why do you have to sneak off and do your bookwork at night?"

"Because it's the only time I get to do it."

"What are you doing during the day?"

"Other work."

"Did you ever stop to think about me or Ems? Or your friends?"

"What do they have to do with me working?"

"Everything. Me and Ems, we're your family. Your blood."

"And?"

"And! I shouldn't have to explain why we want you spending time with us."

"And I shouldn't have to defend myself. I'm providing for my family."

"Is what I provide not enough?"

"Of course it is, but isn't it nice to have more?"

"No, especially if it means that I don't get to see more of you. Ems and I are seeing less and less of you."

"You are not. You see me at dinnertime."

"What about the weekends? What about after dinner? What about in the mornings? What about during the school holidays?"

"Oh, when are they?"

"They've just been. Ems told you about thirty million times."

"No, she didn't." I didn't recall Ems telling me it was the school holidays. Or did she?

"You know, as much as I love you, I hate we don't get to spend any time together anymore."

"I'm spending time with you now."

"Yes, arguing over how much time you don't spend with us."

"Come on, Noah, you know that I'm busy."

"Yes, apparently too busy for us. Look, Carol, I'm sick of this. I'm sick of being taken for granted. I don't want to be a backup guy for you anymore."

"You're not my backup guy, you're my husband."

"Well, a husband implies we make decisions together, and we have done nothing like that about our family for a very long time. I've had enough."

"What do you mean, had enough?"

"I'm leaving. I'm packing my bags and leaving." He turned and left, just like that. I stood up, stunned. Was he hoping to make me chase after him and ask him not to leave? Damned straight he was, and I was running down the hallway after him.

"Noah, wait."

"What?" He glared at me, and I didn't remember seeing that amount of dislike in his face before.

"Don't go."

"I'm sorry, Carol. I've told you so many times that you need to spend time with us, and yet you seem to be in your own world and not realise that I actually meant it."

"I thought you were only trying to get my attention."

"I shouldn't have to 'get your attention'. Me and Ems should be your number one focus, not the business."

"But...but..."

"No buts about it, Carol. I'm sorry. I love you, but I can't keep fighting a business that's more important to you than I am."

I followed him to the door as he opened it.

"Have a think about what is important to you, Carol," he said. He kissed my cheek, then left, closing the door behind him. A cold draft hit me square in the face as it did so.

"Where are you, Mum?" Em's voice pulled me back to reality.

"Sorry, ice cream headache," I said, holding a hand up to my head.

Ems looked at me weirdly. "Okay, well, you finished?"

"Yes," I replied.

"Let's go home."

Chapter Five

January

It had been a long day at the office, and I was tired, grumpy, hot and sticky.

Iona had once again gone on about needing an air conditioner for the office and the workshop, and once again I argued it was an unnecessary expense. The workshop had the large garage doors we could open up. Unfortunately, it didn't allow for any breeze to pass through.

I got home to find Ems was out. A note said she was out for tea with her dad. A gut-wrenching pain swamped my body as I thought of Noah, my Noah, with someone else.

I looked in the fridge and found a bottle of wine and some salad. That would have to do for tea. I poured a glass of wine and sat at the bench. I pulled out my cell phone and went through the news, any notifications on my social media accounts, emails, all while eating the salad out of the bowl with a fork.

The house was so quiet and empty without Ems in it. And without Noah. I sighed.

How had I lost the man of my dreams? By not being here when he needed me.

I took a sip of wine, but it did nothing for me, and with the heat of the day, it tasted off as soon as the chill was gone. I tipped the rest down the sink and went to have a shower.

I stripped off, turned the water on, then studied myself in the mirror. Middle age was catching up with me. I was saggy around the middle. Cellulite rippled up my legs, and some wrinkles lined my face. I wasn't too bad looking, I guess.

Perhaps if I'd kept up my gym membership, I could've been a little more slender but I didn't have enough time in my day to continue with the gym. And the amount of food I ate would probably feed a bird. I had little appetite, especially when things were hectic.

The mirror fogged up, telling me that the shower was probably too hot, so I turned it down and tested the heat.

I got in and let the water sluice over my head, using my hands to wash my face as the water cascaded over my skin. The feeling of scrubbing my hands through my hair was nice as it eased a little tension from my shoulders. I rolled them as I let the tepid water wash over me.

But it still felt hot. It had been a hot day, but even with the door open in the factory, there wasn't enough breeze to cool things down. I had cooked as much as everyone else had, even with all the windows in the office open. I'd let them go early to cool off. The advantages of working for me. I know I can work them hard, but I think I'm a fair boss sometimes.

I lathered up my sponge and washed over my body, under my arms, around my breasts, down my stomach, along my legs. I noticed my pits needed a shave, so I lathered up under there and...what was that?

A lump?

Probably a swollen gland. But it's small, a gland is normally bigger. I scraped my razor over my right armpit and then felt again. Yes, definitely a lump, barely noticeable, but a lump.

Hmm, mental note, talk to Iona.

I finished showering and got out, towel drying myself, and then wiping down the mirror. I felt for the lump again and found it, but I couldn't see anything in my reflection.

Probably nothing to worry about.

Was it?

I shook my head and padded through to my bedroom, the towel wrapped around me, and got out some clean casual clothes, a T-shirt and shorts, no bra. I was over the bra thing. Letting it hang out was my prerogative.

I sat down on the couch and flicked on the television, but nothing was on. I surfed through the channels, but nothing really caught my interest. Something at the back of my brain kept prompting me about the lump under my arm.

I got up to retrieve my phone and wondered what it could be.

Maybe I should research it.

After reading through a few articles, I settled on it being a cyst or an inflamed lymph node, nothing to worry about.

I put my phone down, but I couldn't settle the needling that was going on in my mind.

I was about to search up breast cancer when Ems arrived home. It was nine. Which isn't late for her on a school night.

"How was your day?" I asked. She sat on the couch and curled up with her legs underneath her, her head resting on her hand. She looked like a lanky baby deer, all limbs and nothing else. I used to look like that once too.

"Good. Got an A in English." She rolled her eyes. "Had a maths test, but I passed. Went round to Dad's, had dinner, watched some TV, and I'm back."

"Sounds like an action-packed day." I said, sarcasm rolling off my tongue.

"Yeah, how about you?"

"Busy." It was my standard reply, and she never asked for more details.

She looked at my casual clothes. Normally I came home from work and stayed in my work gear until I went to bed. "What time did you get home?" she asked.

"About four."

She sat up, her eyebrows raised and her eyes wide. "You came home at four? Did everyone leave at four?"

"Yes, it was too hot at the workshop"

Her mouth fell open. "You let everyone go at four?" She reached out a hand and held it against my forehead. "Are you feeling okay?"

I batted it away, grinning at her. "Yes, now, isn't it past your bedtime?"

She rolled her eyes again as she unfolded herself and came over to give me a quick hug and a kiss on the cheek.

"Night, Mum."

"Night, Ems." I heard her disappear down the hallway to her room and the door shut.

I looked at the blank screen on my phone. But my mind wouldn't settle. What if the lump was something more than just a cyst? I seesawed between worry and calm acceptance until, at midnight, I got up and researched it again.

Again, all the signs weren't serious. And I had only just noticed it. I felt for the lump registering it within my mind. It was high in the armpit, near the side of my breast on the right-hand side. It was smaller than a pea, moved a little, but was solid. My mind kept wondering if it was something more.

I vowed to talk to Iona tomorrow.

Chapter Six

February

It was another week before I remembered to tell Iona.

"Can you still feel it?" she asked.

"Yeah," I said, reaching for my underarm. I pointed to where it was, and she felt it too.

"Ah, I think you should go to the doctor about that." She looked at me, her eyebrows drawn down over her eyes.

"It's probably just a cyst," I said, trying to dismiss the sudden chill that crawled up my neck and settled on my scalp.

Iona narrowed her eyes. "How long have you had it?"

"I found it about a week ago."

"What? Honey, you really shouldn't mess with things like that."

"What, it's just a lump," I said. Her tone made me want to shudder.

"It might just be a lump, but what if it's something else?"

"Like?"

"You know"—she leaned forward and whispered—"cancer."

"Ha ha, yeah right, I'm too young to have cancer," I said. "Plus, I don't smoke, I eat relatively healthy, and don't drink heavily." I could list off more things, but the look on Iona's face caused my blood to run cold and sludgy in my veins. So much so, I picked up the phone and immediately rang my doctor's surgery.

"Hello, Peregrine Medical Centre, how can I help?"

"Hi, it's Carol Sawyer here. Can I make an appointment to see Doctor Michelle Roberts, please?"

"Hold one moment while I check…" There was a pause and clicking of nails on a keyboard. "The next available appointment is next Thursday at two fifteen. Is that okay?"

I looked at my diary, flicking over the pages, aware that Iona was staring at me. "I'm free that day, but is there anything sooner?" I asked.

"No, she's full up, but I might be able to book you in with another doctor."

"No, Thursday's good," I said and hung up. "What? It was the soonest I could see my doctor," I responded to Iona's glare.

She folded her arms across her chest. "As long as you go."

I pointed to the date and time. "Just keep that date in mind and make sure I go, if you're so worried," I grumped. I slammed the diary shut and got up from my chair. Iona didn't move as I walked over to the door and opened it, indicating for her to leave.

"I will remind you," she said as she stalked out of the room.

"I know you will," I replied to her retreating back. I shut the door and blew out a breath. Iona had made me nervous about a little insignificant lump.

What's the worst that could happen?

It couldn't be cancer.

I sat in the doctor's surgery, my mind a blur. Once she suggested I needed a mammogram and an ultrasound and muttered the *C* word, my mind switched off. Now, all I could hear was a fuzzy blur of noise.

"Carol? You okay?"

I shook my head and focused my gaze on her. "Huh?"

"You okay?"

"Um, I'm not sure."

"When did you tune out?"

"After mammogram and ultrasound," I muttered.

Doctor Michelle reached across and put her hand on my arm. "It's just a precaution. We need to know what this is. It may just be a cyst, but it doesn't feel right."

"What does it feel like?" I asked. My pulse was racing as I tried to pay attention to what she was saying.

"I don't know. That's why I want the tests to be done."

"And what if it is c-cancer?"

"How about we talk about that once we've had a look? There are a lot of things it could be."

"Okay," I breathed out, not aware I'd been holding it.

"You'll be okay, Carol. You're young. It's a slim chance it's cancer."

I took a deep breath and let it out slowly. "Okay. One step at a time. I can do this."

"Yes, you can." Doctor Michelle looked at me and smiled kindly. "I'll arrange for the mammogram and the ultrasound and I'll let you know when we get the results back what we are looking at, okay?"

"Okay," I said. Now that I'd cleared my head, I felt better. I had a plan, and the doctor was confident that it wasn't cancer. Or that it wasn't too serious. But my mind started into overdrive as I left the office.

If it was cancer, I would have to work out what to do with my business. Would Iona or Noah take it over? Could I leave it to Ems in my will?

Cancer was bad, wasn't it?

You died from cancer.

I thought back over all the years and friends of my parents I knew who had cancer. Most of them had died.

I tried to reason that they had died before innovations had improved treatments, but it was too hard to actually keep that thought going. The fact they had died was all that my mind would cling to.

It was Noah's birthday, and I'd agreed to go out with Ems and Noah for dinner. It was the last thing I felt like doing, but it was his birthday and Ems had requested I come along. My gut was tied up in knots, wondering if I was going to meet his new girlfriend. I put on a smile as I got home from work and we got dressed. We met with Noah at The Pizza Guys.

"How was your day?" Noah asked.

"Good," I responded, trying to keep the smile on my face.

"What's happened at work?" he asked.

"Nothing, why?"

"Well, normally if it was a good day, something had happened at work."

"No, nothing happened."

"What about you?" His eyes narrowed as he focused too much on me.

"I'm fine," I replied.

He turned to look at Ems, and they shared a smile. "Fine...you know what that means?" He wiggled his eyebrows, making Ems giggle.

"What?" I asked, looking between the two of them.

"When a woman say's she's fine, she isn't, and the shit is about to hit the fan," he replied.

"There's nothing wrong, honest," I said, knowing I sounded super defensive.

"Even worse, she's denying it," Ems said, shrugging dramatically, like she was waiting for me to explode.

"Look, we're here to celebrate your birthday, not pick on me, okay?" I said, glaring at Noah.

"Watch out...she's going to blow!" he said, leaning away from me, making Ems giggle even more.

I folded my arms and sat back in the chair, refusing to engage in their stupid drama. I didn't need this today, and I would've loved to have blurted out that I'd been to the doctors today about a lump on my breast, but I didn't want to ruin Noah's day. Besides, he and Ems would have had lots of questions that I didn't have answers for right now.

The doctor's words were still circulating in my head, making me lose track of the conversation that flowed around me, so I let them talk and nodded when they looked over at me, trying to look at least like I knew what they were talking about.

Chapter Seven

February

Here I stood, in the radiology department, about to have my mammogram. I told the technician where the lump was and she felt for it.

"Just so I can get the best picture of it." She squeezed, prodded, and pressed my breasts into awkward shapes to X-ray them. I had to hold still as my breasts were flattened between two cold plates. My cheeks blushed as the technician told me exactly what she was going to do, where she was going to touch me, and what was going to happen. I tried to look like I was comfortable with her actions, but I wasn't. Noah and previous boyfriends were the only ones who had ever touched my boobs, and to have a woman touch them in such a formal and unflattering way made me feel...embarrassed.

When she flattened my left breast, there was a small pinprick of pain, something I hadn't expected.

"Do you get to see the pictures?" I asked.

"Yes," she replied as she fussed around me, getting me to stand in the right position, holding me there so I knew exactly where I was to stay. Being manhandled in such a careful and gentle way felt so odd and contradictory.

"So, you will know if it's cancer or not."

"Yes."

"Has anything come up yet?"

"We won't process the pictures for a couple of days, so I can't tell you now."

Carol's Christmas

I nodded.

"Keep still, please."

I froze in position. And waited as the machine whirred and made noises. It was all clinical and sterile and unemotional. I wanted someone to be nice and assure me that everything was going to be fine, that it was all normal.

"You're doing great," the technician said. It was almost as if she'd been reading my mind.

The poking and pushing had left my breasts feeling tender as I left the clinic. I kept adjusting them in my bra as I walked across the road. I didn't feel violated, just...awkward.

Two days later was the ultrasound, which was a lot more comfortable, although no less embarrassing. I had to strip my top off as the female ultrasound technician smeared goo on my left breast and then pressed the contraption into the flesh. If it wasn't tender before, it was now. She took lots of photos of the area where the lump was. Like the mammogram technician, she couldn't commit to a diagnosis or comment on what she saw. She smiled and told me my doctor would discuss the results with me. This made my awareness of my body suddenly feel more intense. I spent twenty minutes having my boobs photographed, and as I left the hospital, I felt surer that I was going to die than I had the day at the doctor's office. I know that's an exaggeration, but cancer is something that you don't mess with, and I had a feeling that I was going to have a big wake-up call.

The next couple of days at the office were a blur. I didn't talk to Iona much, other than to confirm I'd been to the doctors. I hadn't told her about the mammogram and ultrasound, instead preferring to just let things lie. I was still processing what was happening. I didn't want to talk about it unless it really was nothing.

I tried to drown myself in work, but my mind kept wondering. It kept trying to work through all the different scenarios in my head. Worst case, cancer.

I was young; I was in my early forties, too young for the national breast screening program, and if I hadn't found it now, would it have metastasized in that time and would it be too late?

I normally wouldn't have felt the lump where it was. It was sheet luck that caused me to feel it there that day. I put down my pen and placed my hand underneath my clothing. The lump remained, so the mammogram and ultrasound hadn't squashed, burst, or punctured it, though it felt like they had tried to.

Ugh. I couldn't focus on work. I got up and went into the warehouse to check out what my workers were doing. The noise of the machines whirred as I entered the workspace. The noise cancelled out the thoughts in my brain like white noise. I smiled at Iona as I walked past her workstation and continued into the factory itself.

I talked with some of my staff, commenting on their work. I know I'm tough on them, but they are a good crew. They worked hard, and I had to admit that I was rude to try and make them work between Christmas and New Year. We got the order done, so no harm done.

Doctor Michelle called two days later. She asked me to come in and see her.

Immediately.

She didn't sound panicked, but I knew she would only call me in for an urgent appointment if it was serious. I sat in the waiting room, my heart pounding in my ears, and a whooshing noise filled them every time a name was called by a doctor. Finally, I saw her arrive at the doorway. She looked directly at me and smiled, a sad sort of smile. My chest tightened as she waved me through, and I followed her to her consulting room.

"How are you feeling?" she asked.

I stared at her. "How do you think I'm feeling?" I tried not to sound sassy, but it came out that way.

Dr Michelle nodded. "Okay, I won't beat around the bush. It looks like cancer, but until we take a biopsy, we won't know what kind."

"Couldn't they have done that while I was having the ultrasound?"

"It doesn't work that way. I will refer you to a specialist, and they'll be in touch."

"How long will that take?" My mind filled with questions. "Will the delay in contact make the cancer worse? Will I lose my breast? My hair? What happens next?"

Dr Michelle held her hands up, shaking her head. "Okay, Carol, you need to take a deep breath." She waited until I had attempted to breathe in, which I struggled to do. When I finally let my shoulders drop, she spoke. "Right. The specialist will be in touch with you in the next day or two. They will make an appointment for you and discuss what needs to happen next, like what treatment options are available. Now, I want you to take another deep breath."

I sat staring at her. When she told me to breathe, I breathed in deep. It helped to keep my brain clear enough for her to tell me everything I needed to know for now. She wasn't able to tell me precisely how the treatment would go, but she helped me hear enough to understand.

"You alright to leave? Do you want me to call someone?"

"No, I'm good," I replied.

"Carol, most breast cancers are treatable. Don't let it freak you out."

She knew me so well.

Chapter Eight

February

The specialist called the next day, and I had an appointment the following afternoon. The receptionist told me to bring someone with me as an emotional support person. That freaked me out and made me have a panic attack. Fortunately, Iona came in at that exact moment and got me to sit and breathe.

"What was that all about?" she asked. "Your face is white. Are you alright?" She rubbed my back and helped me to feel more grounded.

I touched my face, which felt cold and clammy. I took a deep breath and slowly let it out. "I have an appointment tomorrow with the specialist."

"What specialist?"

"Cancer specialist."

"*What?*" The word exploded from her mouth and she ceased rubbing my back.

"I had an ultrasound and mammogram, and the lump looks a little like cancer. I have to see a specialist tomorrow. Will you come with me?"

"Of course. How are you feeling?"

I looked up at her. Suddenly, everyone wanted to know how I was feeling. Shocked? Annoyed? Scared? A lot of different emotions. Some, I didn't know their names, flicked through my body, churning my stomach and making my blood run cold. I opened and closed my mouth, unable to really answer without wanting to throw up. I just nodded.

"Oh, honey," she threw her arms around me, hugging me tight. My eyes watered, and before I knew it, I was crying.

All the heartache and terror came out of my eyes in gallons of tears. We stood, holding each other. I was no longer aware of how much time has passed. Finally, I stepped away and grabbed a tissue from the box on my desk, wiping my eyes and blowing my nose. Iona did the same, and I could see that she'd been crying with me. A warmth washed over me. Someone cared.

"So, you want me to come with you?" she asked.

"Would you? Please?"

"Of course. Have you told Ems? Noah?"

"No, I want to know what I'm dealing with first."

"Perhaps you should take one of them."

"No. I don't want to. I don't want to worry Ems, and Noah...well we aren't together, so I don't want to bother him."

"Noah cares about you."

I stare at her. "He loves me so much he moved out and got a girlfriend."

Iona stepped back. "He's got a girlfriend? You wait until I see him."

"You see him?"

Iona at least had the courtesy to blush. "We run into each other occasionally. He's still John's friend, after all."

I remembered all the parties that we went to as a foursome, laughing and enjoying each other's company. I didn't even think that Noah would still be in contact with John.

"Oh..." My heart broke a little more. I was losing Noah, although I had to admit to myself, I lost him a long time ago.

Iona held my hand as we sat in the Doctor's office. Rebecca Nostrum was my oncology doctor, and so far, all I had heard was, "Hi, I'm Rebecca, I'll be your oncology doctor...." before everything buzzed out. I was pleased I'd brought Iona with me. She was taking much more in than I could.

Conversation flowed over me, words like biopsy, operation, chemotherapy, but nothing stuck long enough for me to really comprehend. All I kept thinking was I was too young to die. I had Ems. I wanted to see her grow up, get married, have children, see my grandchildren. I couldn't die now.

Rebecca's smile was genuine, and her head tilted to the side as she contemplated me. Her gaze was soft, and I felt comforted. She took my hands from Iona and held them. Hers were warm, mine felt like ice.

"Okay, Carol, this is going to happen," she said.

I nodded.

"We'll book you in for surgery, take a biopsy and check out the site where the lump is. The biopsy will tell us what course of treatment will be needed next."

"Okay. And then?"

"Shall we just get through the surgery first?"

I nodded. While I liked to know more, I was happy to have her tell me what was going to happen one step at a time. I walked out of the office with a handful of brochures and a head full of fluff. I had asked what I could think of, but as we drove back to the office, questions I should have asked popped in.

"You okay? You're quiet," Iona said as I sat in the passenger seat.

"Trying to absorb it all in."

"Did you hear much of what she said?"

I shook my head, tears threatening to spill. Iona glanced over at me quickly and back to the traffic. "I didn't think you did. You had a vacant expression on your face."

"Almost as soon as she talked about surgery, my mind blanked out." I reached over and patted Iona's arm. "Thanks for being there for me."

"The doctor said that it looks well contained, but until they operate and remove it, they won't know what type of cancer it is. They would do the biopsy once the lump had been removed to determine what follow-up treatment you will need."

I brightened up. "So, I won't need chemo or radiation?"

"She said that chemo would probably be required."

My initial hope deflated. I didn't want to lose my hair, or my breast for that matter.

"Did she say how much of the breast they would take?"

"That would be discussed in the follow-up appointment."

I nodded. Whenever I'd been confronted with news I didn't want to hear, I phased things out. It was a bad habit, one that I formed long before I was an adult. But now, I needed to pull my big girl panties on and actually adult. I mean, I am an adult, but I needed to act like a mature one in stressful situations.

"You going to tell Ems and Noah?"

"Not today."

"Why not?"

"Why should I? I'm still coming to grips with it myself. I'm still trying to wrap my head around what is going on without someone else asking me questions that I have no answers to."

"You should have been listening then."

"I know! God, Iona, it's not like I didn't try."

Iona sat in silence, staring out the window. She knew what I was like, had known I found some situations tough. When Noah had left, I blanked out his voice as he picked up his bag and left the house. All I remember is a buzzing sound in my ears and him looking at me longingly. His shoulders slumped, and his hand reached for the door. Then, in slow motion, he opened it, and walked out, shutting it behind him without looking back. My heart broke at the sound of the latch clicking shut.

"I'm sorry, Carol."

"I know, I'm sorry too. I don't mean to snap at you. You've stuck by me when everyone else has left. You've taken a lot of my crap on board. You're right. I need to face up to this. It's going to be hard, and I have to stop switching off."

"I'm here when you need me, you know that."

"And I appreciate you for it," I said, smiling at her. The tears finally spilled as my chest emptied itself of the emotions that had filled it up. The anguish, pain, anger, heartache, fear and disappointment poured out as I searched for a tissue through my handbag.

"It's going to be okay," she said, putting her hand on my arm.

I sniffled as I dabbed at my eyes, trying not to let the mascara run into them. "I'm going to put that on your gravestone," I said, laughing through the tears.

Iona looked shocked for a moment before bursting out laughing. "And yours is going to say, 'Just one more, come on, just one more'."

Laughter filled the car with a positive energy, and by the time we arrived back at work, my face was back to normal, although perhaps a little flushed, and my eyes were still watery.

"Thank you," I said to Iona before we got out of the car.

"It's okay." Iona smiled.

Chapter Nine

March

Upon further thought, I decided I needed to let Ems and Noah know. Normally it was Ems's night at Noah's, so I rang Noah and asked if I could take him and Ems out for dinner. He was immediately suspicious. "Why?"

"Can I not take my ex and daughter out for dinner?" I asked.

"You normally have an ulterior motive," he stated. And he was right this time too.

"I just want to spend time with my favourite people," I said. "If you don't want to, that's fine, but I will be at Broadtree Lane for dinner at six thirty. See you there." I hung up. It was rude, but I didn't want to talk further and blab to Noah exactly what was happening, because the longer I talked to him, the more likely it was that I would just blurt it out. And I wanted to tell them together.

But on second thoughts, maybe I should tell him first so he can help Ems adjust. Because she will take it hard. And I was struggling enough as it was without trying to keep her positive.

I picked up my phone, and just as I was about to dial Noah, the phone rang. It was him.

"I'm sorry," he said.

"So am I," I replied.

"Why?"

"I have an ulterior motive." I sighed. "Look, Noah, I've been to the doctors and had a mammogram and ultrasound..." I heard his intake of breath. "I have to have surgery, because I've found a lump in my breast."

"Oh, Carol, are you okay?" The tenderness in his voice nearly undid me. I had to concentrate on him instead of the pain in my throat.

"I'm coping," I said. Noah would know exactly what I meant. I was barely clinging to any attempt at sanity.

"Okay, so you were going to tell us at dinner?"

"Yes, but then I thought it was probably best if we tell Ems together because she's staying with you tonight. I'm not up to really talking about it at the moment."

"Right. She might want to stay with you tonight when she finds out."

"I'd like to have tonight at home to process it myself, if that's alright. I only found out, like, an hour ago."

"Did Iona go with you?"

"Yes, I asked her to."

"You could have asked me." His voice was soft, full of emotion.

"I know." A tear trickled down my cheek. "But I don't want to interfere in your new life." My heart cracked again. One day, it would just split apart, and I would have nothing left. I missed Noah, but he wasn't mine anymore.

"I get it." He sighed. "Okay, I'll make sure we're there tonight, and she'll come home with me."

"Thank you," I said, swiping the tear off my cheek, hoping that he couldn't tell I was crying, but he'd know. He always knew.

"See you tonight," he said.

"Noah...ah...I..." I couldn't find the words to express how scared I was.

"Hey, it's going to be okay," he replied.

"Yeah...okay. Thanks." Putting my head in my hands, I said goodbye and hung up the phone. I grabbed some tissues from the box and blew my nose and wiped my eyes. Had to keep the mascara in place. I glanced in the mirror, hitched my shoulders up, plastered a sunny, cheerful face on, and went out into the factory.

At six fifteen, I was sitting in a booth at the back of the restaurant. It was a lovely little place. They served steak just like the old days, carpet bags, rich casseroles, smothered in garlic butter and mushrooms, anyway you liked it. It used to be our favourite restaurant until things got too busy at work. I remember how Friday nights used to rock here, have an early tea, a few drinks, then the restaurant cleared, and it was a dance bar. Those were the days.

I'd grabbed a glass of Pinot noir from the bar and took a sip, glancing over the menu. I didn't have to wait long. Ems pranced up to the table and pecked me on the cheek, then shuffled around to sit at the head of the table. Noah hugged me a little longer than normal and kissed my cheek. My heart splintered again as I nodded and sat down. He sat opposite me, staring at me.

"How was your day?" I asked Ems.

"Oh, the usual, good, bad and everything in between."

I smiled at her, then looked at Noah. "And yours?"

"Couldn't have been any worse than yours," he said outright. His face was serious, and he was staring into my eyes like he was looking into my soul, trying to find the cancer in there.

"What?" Ems asked, glancing at us. I tried to glare at Noah without Ems seeing, but it was hard with her sitting between us.

"I have some news for you," I said, reaching out and taking one of her hands. "I found a lump in my breast a couple of weeks ago. I've been to the doctor, done some tests, and seen a specialist today."

"You didn't say anything," Ems said, her face going pale as I spoke.

"I didn't want to worry you."

"Well, I'm worried now."

"I know." I patted her hand, and Noah reached over and put his on top of mine. "It's cancer."

Ems took a sharp breath in. "Are you going to die?"

My stomach turned to stone. I felt clammy, and my mouth went dry. I had a mouthful of water.

"I'm hoping not to," I continued. "I'll have an operation soon; it will determine what type of cancer it is and what treatments will follow."

Ems's distraught face made my chest tighten.

"You knew, Dad?" She turned to him, her words accusatory.

"Mum rang to ask us to dinner. She told me then."

"Honey"—I had to remove my hands, they were feeling clammy, but Noah continued to hold Ems's hand—"It's difficult to process at the moment. I've only just found out myself. I don't have any answers for you right now."

"I'm coming to the next appointment," she stated. I stared at her defiant face, the determination and hope there. Those were things I needed. I tried to smile at her, but my face felt more contorted. I stopped trying and sighed.

"You'll continue to go to school and study hard, and I will give you a blow-by-blow account after every appointment. Okay?" I said. Ems narrowed her eyes as she studied me and her father. Those eyes were so familiar, the grit and determination in them, the same as her father's.

"Okay," she said.

I nodded, because I really didn't want to discuss this any further than I already had.

"So, dinner anyone?" I pointed to the menus on the table.

"How can you be so cold about this?" Ems asked.

"I'm not, I'm trying to get through this meal so I can go home and try to figure things out."

"I'm coming home with you tonight," Ems said.

"No," Noah and I said together. She stared between us again.

"No, we'll let Mum go home and process, and hopefully she can talk to you more tomorrow after school," he said.

"Seriously, honey, I've only just found out. I need to go home, have a good cry and work out what is happening next."

"I want to be with you." I could see the tears shimmering in her eyes.

"Oh, baby, just one night, that's all I'm asking," I said, blinking rapidly to dispel the excess water in my own. I could see her shoulders hunch and she was prepared to fight, but after looking at her dad, she turned back to me.

"You'll be okay? You won't do anything stupid?"

"Of course not. I have you to answer to." I smiled, trying to make it reach my eyes, but I could tell from her reaction that it didn't.

"Look, I'll be okay, honest."

Ems reluctantly nodded. She wiggled closer to me on the bench seat, and I could feel her body warmth on my side. It was the closest thing I would get to a hug in public.

Chapter Ten

March

I got home, and the place felt empty without Ems, but I'd wanted this quiet moment for a reason. I had a phone call to make. I needed to tell Mum. That was going to be the hardest discussion. Mum always looked on the bright side of life, but anything like cancer could send her into a tailspin, even if it was treatable. Mum retired Tauranga when Dad passed. Her sister, Anthea, lived there, So they moved in together. And those two were something to behold. They were always laughing and carrying on like everything was a joke. They didn't appear to have a care in the world.

It took a bit of persuading myself to pick up the phone and dial her number.

"Hello, darling," her voice purred down the phone. "To what do I owe the honour?"

"Do I need an excuse to ring you?" I tried to keep humour in my tone, but with the news I had to share, it wasn't easy.

"You normally only ring when there's a disaster going on in your life," she replied. I closed my eyes, reminding myself that she is my mother. A woman who gave birth to me and is supposed to care about me. But she was probably right. I pinched the bridge of my nose.

"Aren't I allowed to ring you when things are good?"

"Oh, are they?"

"Ah, yes?"

"They aren't, are they? Is Ems okay?"

"Ems is fine. Noah is fine."

"What about you?"

"I...ah...went to the doctors, and I had to have a mammogram and an ultrasound, and I have breast cancer." The words spilled out of me in a flurry of sounds. I heard her sharp intake of breath.

"You okay?" she asked. "Is it treatable? Are you having surgery?"

"I'm fine, Mum. It's all in hand," I replied. It didn't feel like it, but I didn't need her overreacting or, heaven forbid, offer to come down and help.

"I have surgery coming up, and then I'll have chemotherapy and radiation after that."

"Oh dear, do you want me to come down?"

And there it was. The last thing I needed was Mum coming down and trying to help. We would be fine for a couple of days, then we would start niggling at each other, and then we would start arguing. It would turn into chaos.

"No, Mum, it's all good. I have plenty of people here to look out for me."

"Oh, okay." I could hear the disappointment in her voice.

"Mum, I'm okay. This is going to be okay."

"If you're sure."

"I'm sure. The doctor told me it's all in hand, and breast cancer is much more treatable than it was back in the day." I don't know if I said that for Mum's sake or my own. But things had advanced even in the last twenty years.

"Okay, so other than that, how are you?"

"I'm doing okay. Broke the news to Noah and Ems earlier tonight."

"How'd they take the news?"

"Ems is upset. Noah is stoic, but he'll support Ems."

"What about you? Will he be there for you too?"

"Yes, yes, and I have Iona, so I'm all good."

"As long as you have everything taken care of."

"Yes, I do. Thanks, Mum."

"I'm just a phone call away if you need me."

"I know." I sighed quietly, knowing the worst of the conversation was over. We spoke briefly about how mad Aunty Anthea was, how Tauranga was treating her, and what she'd been up to.

I hung up the phone twenty minutes later and breathed out, feeling my shoulders relax. It was a relief to get that phone call out of the way. I knew my conscience was clear now. Mum knew, so there was no comeback later on. I know that in similar circumstances, Mum wouldn't tell me until after she'd had surgery and chemo if she were in the same situation, but if I did that to her, my life wouldn't be worth living. Even though I was a full-grown adult, she still treated me like a wayward teenager if I kept anything from her.

I went to the cupboard to see if I had any red wine left, but it was all gone. There was no open wine in the fridge, either.

I didn't feel like going out to get any alcohol, so I decided I didn't need any to settle my nerves. Perhaps an early night might help.

I climbed into bed, the phone call still in my head. Mum had been angry when I'd told her that Noah and I had split. And it wasn't anger at Noah. Mum loved Noah. It was all my fault that we'd split, but he was the one that left, not me. It sometimes felt like I couldn't do anything right.

Mum had worked when I was little. Everyone else at school had mums that stayed at home and baked and cooked. Mum did those things, too, but she also worked because Dad never seemed to hold down a job, so it fell on her shoulders to do everything. Dad just sat on his chair, reading the newspaper jobs list, then he'd go out, do something for a week or two, then find it too hard and would come home again. There was no such thing as a benefit back then, and Mum earned way less than Dad did. I never knew we were poor, but I always remember the hard work that Mum put in, day and night, to make sure that we didn't miss out on anything. I guess that's where I get my attitude to hard work and making things happen.

When Dad died, Mum decided that she'd done enough for me and headed north to be with her sister. I'd felt the sting of rejection when she'd left, but I put that down to the fact that she no longer had to put food on my table and was off to enjoy herself. I didn't deny that she deserved that. It just would've been nice to have her closer. She had missed out on a lot of Ems growing up, but I guess she's doing what makes her happy now.

I just wish I could be happy for her too.

Chapter Eleven

April

My surgery date was the same day as my birthday. What a day to celebrate.

Ems decided that since we couldn't celebrate my birthday on the day, we should do something the weekend before.

"Look, honey, I'd just as happily not do anything."

"Mum, it's your birthday. We need to celebrate it."

I sighed, because we didn't need to celebrate anything. I was only another year older.

"Come on, we need something positive to do," she whined.

"And my operation isn't positive enough?"

"That's not what I meant. I mean...What if...this...is your last..." She ducked her head down, and I could see her face pale. I moved over to her and put my arms around her. "It won't be my last birthday, okay?"

She sniffed and reached her arms around me, holding me tightly. It felt nice to be holding her, because we didn't really hug much anymore.

"I don't want to have a party," I said, trying to console her. She lifted her head and smiled at me, her eyes shining with unshed tears.

"How about we all go out for a family dinner then?"

"Who's all? I'd rather it was just you and me."

"And Dad?" She looked me in the eye, because we were the same height now. When did that happen? She was waiting for my reaction, and while my insides jumped for joy, I kept my face neutral.

"Yeah, I suppose," I said, sounding like it was a hassle.

"Cool, I'll ring him now." she said.

And that is how we ended up here at the Italian Place for dinner, two days before my operation.

"Happy birthday," Noah said, kissing my cheek and giving me a card. I smiled as I opened it, laughing at the joke card he'd given me.

"All good for Tuesday?" he asked.

"Yeah, pre-surgery all done. Just need to turn up in the morning."

"You got a ride?"

"Yeah, Iona is picking me up," I said, noting how his eyebrows dipped down over his eyes and a frown pulled at his lips. "First up on the list, so need to be there bright and early." I said, trying to sound bright, while my insides were shaking so much, I thought I'd be sick.

"Best of luck with the surgery then," he said, sitting back in his seat.

"Thanks. Shall we go ahead and order now?" I asked, looking at Ems and Noah. I didn't really feel like eating, so I ordered a salad. Noah watched me pick at my meal and push it around my plate.

When Ems excused herself to go to the bathroom, Noah leaned over, resting his hand on my arm. I could feel the heat rush up my body, but I tried not to show how his touch affected me.

"Are you really okay?"

"Of course," I replied, but my smile faltered. "I'm nervous."

"I thought so. It'll be okay."

"Will it?"

"Of course. The surgeon is a professional."

"Do you know her?"

"Well, no. But she wouldn't be performing the surgery unless she knew what she was doing."

"What if it's worse than it looks?"

"It won't be," he said, rubbing his thumb across the fabric of my shirt. I wished he was touching my bare skin.

"How can you be so sure?"

"I don't. I just need to believe that it'll all turn out fine."

I sighed. "I hope so."

"You'll be fine. Ems and I will be there when you wake up."

"I'd rather..." I was going to say I didn't want them there, but they'd argue with me, so I nodded instead. "Okay."

His hand moved to hold mine. His hand felt warm compared to mine.

"It'll be fine. You've got this," he said, as if the words alone would instil confidence within me. I nodded, because the lump in my throat prevented me from speaking.

Ems came back to the table and looked pointedly at our hands. I took my hand away, putting it in my lap, feeling my insides cool down. I didn't need to have these feelings right now. I needed to focus on me and getting through the surgery.

My stomach was twisting up with every passing hour. I drove home with Ems watching me closely.

"Are you and Dad..."

"No, Ems. We're not getting back together. Your dad was trying to encourage me. That's all."

"Oh."

Her small brief comment said it all. And I felt her pain because it was a hollow feeling that was at the very core of my being. Had been there since Noah had left. I wished with all of my heart that he'd come back, but he kept telling me actions were louder than words, and that I hadn't made any changes to show that I really was serious about wanting him back. I tried, I called, I talked, I pleaded, I begged. I tried working less, spending more time at home, but then work would suck me back in again.

"Your Dad made his decision. He isn't coming back."

"You haven't exactly tried, Mum."

I couldn't believe I was hearing this from her. "I have tried. I did everything he asked, but he isn't back yet."

"Mum, you spend more time at work now than you ever did."

"I've tried to cut back, but the more I cut back, the more work I need to do. Ems, you need to see this from my point of view."

"Try seeing it from mine." She crossed her arms over her chest. The silence thickened the tension in the car, and when we got home, she went straight to her room without saying goodnight.

"Goodnight, Mum. Goodnight, Ems, hope you sleep well. I will, Mum, you too," I said as I walked into the kitchen, turning on the light.

What Ems said stung. Was there some truth in it? I tried to be a good mum; I tried to be a good wife. I worked hard; I did everything that was asked of me.

Was I doing too much?

Chapter Twelve

April

On the day of the surgery, I opened the door to see Noah standing there.

"Oh." I took a step back. "I was expecting Iona," I said, not hiding my disappointment. If she didn't turn up soon, we'd be late to the hospital.

"That's why I'm here. *I'm* taking you."

"Why?"

"Why not?" he asked, picking up my overnight bag and heading out the door without any questions. I stood stunned in the hallway with my handbag over my shoulder. I picked up the keys from the key rack and followed him outside, locking the door behind me. I climbed into his car and sat there, staring at him.

"Seriously, why are you here?" I asked. For the life of me, I couldn't figure out why he wanted to take me to the hospital.

"I told Iona I would take you," he said, starting the car and heading out onto the road towards the hospital, a thirty-minute drive away.

An awkward silence followed as I sat fidgeting with my fingers, trying to calm the butterflies that were dipping and diving in my stomach. I had wanted to sit in the car and just breathe, but with Noah beside me, it was hard to focus on breathing. He was my ex-husband, the man I still loved. My insides tightened more, and I found it harder to relax with him in such proximity to me.

"You alright?" he asked.

"Not really."

"Why?"

I stared at him. "I'm having surgery in about an hour's time."

He smiled. And I felt my eyebrows draw down as my heart rate increased. "What's so funny?"

"Nothing. Of course you're nervous. What can I do to help?"

"Stop talking to me."

"Why?"

"Oh, dear God! I need to relax."

"You can relax around me," he said.

"No, I can't. You're my ex-husband, I love you, and you don't love me—"

"I never said I didn't love you."

"Then why did you leave?" Before he spoke, I could hear the buzzing start in my ears. I took a deep breath through my nose and focused on Noah.

"I left because you had no time for me or our marriage."

"I—" I shut my mouth. I had stopped spending time with Noah, but I didn't think I'd been neglecting our marriage. I always believed Noah wanted the same things as me, wanted me to succeed in my business.

"But you always supported and encouraged me to make the most of the business."

"Yes, I did, but then you got so involved with it that you didn't have time for me. We would come together in the evenings, and you were too tired to actually do anything. We barely made love, and even on the weekends, you were so focused on work or working that we didn't do any family things. It was always Ems and I that went out and had picnics or played tennis. Remember when we used to go out and have dinner, then stay out and dance for a couple of hours? That all stopped once the business took off. You just didn't know when to stop."

"I couldn't stop. If I stood back, the business would fail."

"Would it?"

I opened my mouth, but I couldn't answer that question. "It's my business. I can't let it fail."

"Nobody is going to let it fail."

"But if I'm not running it..."

"Iona is more than capable, and you have amazing staff. That place hums."

"Only because I'm there making sure that it does."

"And at Christmas time? You stressed yourself out working over the Christmas and New Year period when your staff would've been more than capable of getting it done in the two weeks available in January."

"You don't know that."

"I actually do. Remember, I helped you start the business, helped you employ the staff. That place will survive without you. But will you survive without the business?"

I looked away from him. The familiar buzz filled my head, and I tuned him out. My heart was racing like I was two breaths away from a panic attack. I took a deep breath in through my nose and let it out through my mouth. I took another breath, slow, deep, even. Blew it out, slow, deep and even. The buzzing cleared from my hearing. I put my head back against the headrest, closed my eyes, and breathed in and out, slowly drawing the air into the bottom of my lungs. I opened my eyes and found that we were at the hospital. The butterflies swooped and dived around my empty stomach. I didn't want to bring anything up. I hadn't had anything to eat, so it would only be bile. The thought made my mouth water, and I felt hot and clammy. I opened the car door and tried to get out, but I couldn't. The car held me fast.

"You need to undo your seatbelt." Noah said as he clicked the button. I tumbled out of the car and sat on the road, hyperventilating. Noah rushed around to me and picked me up off the ground. "Just breathe."

"That's what I'm trying to do," I said, angry at myself for being such a mess. It's only an operation. It's not like its lifesaving or anything...but it was. I had cancer. I needed to have this thing removed. Along with half of my breast.

Noah took my hand and squeezed it. I squeezed his back, and my shoulders dropped and my breathing evened out.

"You've got this, honey," he said, smiling at me. I attempted to smile back, but I wasn't very successful. I think it was more of a grimace. It felt like that anyway.

We were silent as he walked with me to the surgical unit and got me settled in to the room. I'd been presented with a fancy paper gown, which I struggled to get into without ripping it. I sat on the bed, my stomach twisting up in knots. I was the first in for surgery, so I didn't have a long wait.

"Hi there." Rebecca smiled as she entered the room. She had on a green gown, and a matching cap.

"This is Noah, Noah, Rebecca, my oncology doctor," I introduced them. Noah reached out his hand, and his face lit up with his boyish smile. A burning sensation raced through my chest as I watched my *ex*-husband interact with another female. Now my gut felt like concrete as Noah smiled and shook Rebecca's hand.

"Nice to meet you, Noah. Are you ready for this, Carol?"

"No."

Rebecca laughed. "You're okay. I've done this before, and we'll know what to do next once we're done with today." She turned back to Noah. "She'll be back out in a couple of hours if you want to come back later."

Noah smiled at her. He leaned forward and kissed my cheek. "You've got this," he whispered.

Chapter Thirteen

April

Blips and beeps came into my consciousness before I noticed more noise. Bustling of feet, curtains being moved, crisp bed linen crumpling, whispers of voices. I blinked my eyes, aware that I wasn't at home, but unsure where I was. The room was bright, white, sterile. The ceiling was panelling filled with hundreds of holes. I rolled my head to the side, aware that my mouth felt like I'd eaten a pillow's worth of cotton wool.

"Hey," a soft voice next to me said. I looked around in what felt like slow motion and saw Ems.

"Hey," I said, smiling at her. I lifted an arm that felt heavier than usual and tried to reach out to her. She took my hand and held it.

"How you feeling?"

"Like I'm still asleep." I over-pronounced each word. "Drink?" I asked. She passed a cup with a straw towards me and lifted my head to take a small sip. The water tasted like the finest champagne in the world. I tried not to drink too much, but it slaked my thirst and hunger.

I handed the cup back and lay back on the pillow. That small expenditure of energy cost me. I closed my eyes. I felt her warm hand pick mine up again, and I squeezed her hand in response. It was comforting to know that someone I loved was there for me.

"Shouldn't you be at school?"

"School's finished."

I was too tired to look at the clock to see if she was right. She would be, though. Ems didn't normally lie to me.

"How was school?"

"Rough."

"Why?"

"You were in surgery."

"I wasn't in there long."

"No, but you've taken a while to come out of the anaesthetic."

"Have I?" I really didn't care. I kind of liked the almost euphoric state that I was in. My brain didn't register any pain. If I didn't move, I felt light as a feather, floating. It was only when I moved my limbs they felt like concrete.

"The nurses have come in and checked on you nearly every hour."

"Oh, they worried?"

"Not really."

I nodded, but the movement was jerky and awkward.

"The surgery went okay. They got the lump and some surrounding tissue out."

"You talked to the doctor?"

"Yes, she called in not long after I got here. She said she'd call in later to talk to you."

"Okay."

"Dad was here earlier."

"He brought me in."

"I know."

There was silence, just the movement of her thumb rubbing over my hand. The motion was enough to send me off to la-la land again.

I heard more voices this time, and I opened my eyes to Noah, Iona, Ems and Dr Rebecca standing around the bed, talking in hushed tones.

"I'm awake," I said, trying to sit up in the bed.

"Good. You had a good rest," Rebecca stated.

"Hmm," I said, because I did actually feel rested.

"Everything went well. We removed the tumour and five lymph nodes and some of the surrounding tissue. The tumour was bigger than expected, and we did a partial mastectomy. The biopsy is in at the lab, and we put a port-a-cath in while we were there. That's to get the chemo into the area that needs treatment."

"Chemo?" My blood cooled in my body at the sound of that. "Was it worse than you thought?"

"No, chemo was always going to happen. We need to know what ongoing treatment we can offer you once chemo and radiation are done."

"Oh," I looked up at the four faces staring back at me. My brain was full of fluffy clouds, not much was penetrating at the moment, blissful sleep was beckoning me back into its gentle arms.

This time, I woke up and felt more awake. I looked around the room and found Ems sitting on my bed, still holding my hand, and working her cell phone with the other.

"Hey, sunshine," I said. I tried to sit up, but my elbows hurt. Bloody starch! I scooted myself up and reached for the drink. Ems read my mind and grabbed it for me, bringing it closer.

"Thank you," I said. Things were sore, not aching, but I was aware of some discomfort. I put the cup back and lifted the oh-so-fashionable hospital gown. The bandages covered everything, so I couldn't see what had been done.

"The doctor said the operation went well."

"Yes, I remember her being here at some stage. What time is it?"

"It's after six."

"Wow, the anaesthetic kicked my butt."

"Yes, it did." Ems smiled at me. "You feeling okay?"

"Yes, no, I don't know. Tender."

"There are more painkillers available if you want them. I can let a nurse know."

"No, I'm good. Why are you still here?"

"I didn't want to leave you alone."

"Oh, Ems, I'm okay. Seriously, nothing is going to happen to me."

"I know, I just...I wanted to make sure you came through surgery, okay?"

I reached out and put my arm on Ems. "I love you," I said.

"I love you too, Mum."

I pulled her down so she was lying on the bed, resting her head on my good shoulder. It was a long time since we had done this, and it felt nice and comforting to know that my daughter loved me and would still hug me occasionally.

There was a gentle knock at the door and Ems pushed herself off me as Noah came in.

"Hey," he said.

"Hi." I smiled at him. His hair was shaggy, like he'd been raking his fingers through it, and his eyes looked tired.

"How you feeling?" he asked as he put his hands in his pockets and stood at the end of the bed.

"Like a bicycle has run over me," I replied, trying not to laugh. "It's not too bad, actually."

"You were certainly out of it for a while. Had us a little worried."

"Worried? You guys worried about me?" I wasn't sure whether to be shocked or laugh. Nobody ever worried about me before. "I'm okay. I probably needed the rest, nervous energy and all that stuff."

"Yeah, okay. Anyway, Doc said things went well. She's pleased with the operation, pretty sure she got everything."

"Yeah, Ems said she'd been. I kind of remember her being here," I replied. I also vaguely recollected her talking about chemo and radiation as well. But that was for future Carol to worry about. Today, I woke up without a lump in my breast, and hopefully it hadn't spread.

Chapter Fourteen

April

I felt a little stiff after surgery, and when I moved, there was a slight pinching under my armpit. After a few days, Rebecca carefully unwound the bandages from my chest and it was the first time I got to see the results of the surgery. My breast looked like it had caved in. I had expected a long line of stitches running along an angry red scar, but she'd done the surgery through the nipple, leaving minimal scarring. There was a small tube coming out underneath my breast, which was a drain to let fluid leak out. What kind of liquid, I didn't know.

But it was just the lack of boob that concerned me the most. Most of the left-hand side of the breast underneath my arm was gone.

I hadn't realised how feminising a breast was until you don't have half of one. The bruising was the scariest part; it looked like I'd done ten rounds with Mike Tyson, and I certainly hadn't won.

"The wound is healing nicely. Everything seems to have settled well." She gently touched the breast and smiled at me. "Feels weird, doesn't it?"

I nodded. By the time I'd had surgery, I'd gotten used to having my breasts on display, especially for Rebecca. I'd even got used to them being touched by a woman, something I hadn't thought of or felt comfortable with before. She touched the area around the nipple with such a delicate touch.

"Okay, pop your clothes back on, and I'll see you next door." She left me to get dressed, and when I was done, I swept back the curtain and sat next to Iona.

"Everything looks wonderful. The scar will fade with time." "It's healing nicely," Rebecca said. She looked at her notes.

"We will start chemotherapy in six weeks to allow for the healing to be mostly done."

My ears started buzzing. I had to force myself to focus and listen to what she was saying. "Do I have to have chemotherapy?"

"Yes, it will help ensure that we destroy all the cancer."

"I thought you got it all." I clenched my hands tightly in my lap as I spoke. Rebecca leaned forward and touched my hands.

"I'm pretty sure I did, and the biopsy confirms this, but we need to make sure that there are no more mutated cells that could make the cancer come back."

I nodded, trying to take it all in. Science hadn't been my forte at school. "Okay, so how long will the chemo take?"

"About twenty sessions, which is twenty weeks."

My eyes bulged as I turned to look at Iona. She rested her hand on my arm and looked at me reassuringly.

"It's okay. Your friends and family will be there for you," she said, but it wasn't that. Twenty weeks was a long time to leave my business alone. I needed it to validate me as a person. If it failed…

"Then you have radiation on top of that, again to ensure that the area is cancer free."

I gulped, my face feeling hot and cold all at once. "What else did the biopsy say?"

"You have the best kind of cancer to have."

"There's a good kind?"

"Not a good kind, no. But this one responds well to treatment, and you'll be on a hormone-based treatment for the next five years," Rebecca said.

Five years! I had a five-year timeframe before I could be considered cancer free. I shuddered as I tried to work out how I really felt. Anaesthetic had messed up my brain. Now I had to focus on the longer term.

"When do I start chemo?" I asked.

"Six weeks, so about mid-June," Rebecca said. I nodded, realising I had six weeks to get things sorted and organised. "You've already got the port-a-cath in, so you're ready to go."

Rebecca leaned forward and touched an area just below my collarbone. "The chemotherapy will be in a liquid form. It will be put into this port-a-cath and delivers the liquid directly to the site."

I reached up to where she touched, and I could feel something small and foreign sitting under the skin. How were they going to get the chemo into that if it was already under my skin?

"I'll get a radiation nurse to get in contact with you and talk you through the next part, okay?" She must have read my face, because she lowered her head and stared at me. "It's going to be okay. You've got this."

I laughed. It wasn't a funny 'ha ha' laugh, more a sarcastic laugh. "I've heard that so much lately, I'm thinking it's my new motto," I replied. Rebecca and Iona laughed, but I wasn't finding it funny at all.

"Right," I said, nodding, feeling like one of those dorky dogs in the backs of cars. If I kept nodding, I thought my head might fall off.

I got home that night to an anxious Ems. "How did it go?" she asked.

"Good, it seems she got all the cancer, but I have to have some chemotherapy and radiation."

"If they got it all, why do you need chemo?" she asked. She reminded me so much of myself.

"To be sure they have it, and to stop any other mutant genes from forming cancer."

"But if they got it all, why would there be any mutant genes?"

"I don't know, honey. All I know is in six weeks' time, I start chemotherapy."

Ems blinked rapidly and looked pale. She reached out and touched my hair. "You'll lose this," she said.

I hadn't thought of that. I wasn't totally worried about the chemo, but I loved my hair, the fiery red colour. The way it curled around my face. Most people hated curly hair, but I loved mine.

"Yes, I might," I said. My mouth felt like cotton wall was packed inside it

"I'll shave mine too," Ems said, running her fingers through her own red locks. She straightened hers, but it was almost a strawberry blonde colour. "I could donate mine to have a wig made," she said.

"Hey, how about we both do that?" I suggested. I'm sure that they could do something with my own frizzy hair.

"I'd like that. When do you want to do it?"

"How about we do it just before I start chemo? That way, we can make sure it's a lot longer."

Ems's eyes lit up. "Good idea. I might see if there are other girls at school who want to do it too. Maybe we could raise money?"

"That's a good idea, sweetie," I said, hugging her, but I still had to get used to the idea that I would lose another part of my femininity—my hair.

Carol's Christmas

I was back on my feet a couple of weeks after surgery and back at work. How could I not? They needed me to keep them going and to get the next order out. My restrictions limited my activities, and I dreaded the upcoming chemotherapy. The port-a-cath sat in my chest, which was awkward and strange to work around. I hated showering and seeing what had happened to my breast. The doctor said there are prosthetics you can get to fill out the breast, but to be honest, I don't really have much of a chest anyway, and enhancing it seems silly since I don't have a partner, and the chances of finding another partner was slim, because of work commitments.

I found that getting closer to treatment, I kind of wanted Ems around more, but she seemed to never be there when I needed her. It wasn't like she was at her dad's more than usual; she wasn't. It just felt like it.

In the weeks after surgery, Iona and a couple of other staff members brought 'spare' meals to work. They'd been made specifically for Ems and I. To start with, it felt awkward accepting the meals, but after the third week, I realised it was nice to not have to race home to cook a meal, and I could sit and relax for a few minutes before reheating the dishes provided.

Often, I woke up to Ems wandering into the lounge.

"Sorry, I nodded off," I said, sitting up on the couch, stretching out my neck and shoulders from the scrunched position I'd fallen asleep in.

"It's okay. How are you feeling?"

My pet peeve question. I sighed. "Fine." It seemed enough to keep her from asking more.

I went to sit up and make room on the couch for her.

"Don't worry, Mum. I'm all good. The casserole is in the oven. I'll check on it soon." And she was off to her room, I presume, to do homework.

I sighed as I tried to find a comfortable position to sit in. I wasn't used to being so tired, and I felt like I wasn't getting much done. I had to be less lazy and more onto it. It was since the surgery that I found myself dozing off in the late afternoons after work. It seemed to take forever to get the anaesthetic out of my system.

Christmas Present

"Come in!" exclaimed the Ghost
"Come in! and know me better, man!"
Scrooge entered timidly, and hung his head before this Spirit. He
was not the dogged Scrooge he had been; and though the Spirit's
eyes were clear and kind, he did not like to meet them.
"I am the Ghost of Christmas Present," said the Spirit. "Look
upon me!

A Christmas Carol
Charles Dickens

Chapter Fifteen

May / June

My guts churned as I waited at the hairdresser's. It was mid-May, and Ems was with me, along with five other college-age girls all giggling, whispering and pointing at their phones. Ems had got them and their parents to consent to have their hair cut and donated to a wig-making company for cancer patients. She had also raised money for the Breast Cancer Association through the school, making her a hero in my eyes, but then I'm biased. Her and I would be last to have our hair done. All week, I'd been staring at my hair in the mirror, then hiding it under a scarf to see how I would look without hair, but it was hard to tell with the mass that sat underneath the scarf, bulking it up.

Now, I sat in the hairdresser's. Reality was really hitting home. Nerves made my stomach hard, and I had to focus on something else to keep my lunch down. I'd lost my appetite during the week, which I knew would be hard when it came to chemo, but I wasn't hungry. Weight had melted off me in the last two weeks, and I already looked really thin. I looked like a cancer patient, although I wasn't. Or was I?

The hairdresser called up the first two girls, put their long hair in ponytails, then cut them off. They opted for a short style, while the next two girls had their heads fully shaved. The next two opted for a variation of shaved and short.

Then it was our turn. Ems held my hand as we sat in the chairs, capes draped around our shoulders. We smiled at each other in the mirrors as the hairdressers scraped up Ems's hair into a high ponytail, and my hairdresser wrangled my frizzy red hair into some form of ponytail. The hairdressers clinked their scissors together as Ems and I continued to hold hands, squeezing each other in support.

I closed my eyes as I felt the first snips cut through. I kept them closed until I felt no more cutting, and the hairdresser held up my hair like a triumphant trophy. Buzzing hit my ears, and I had to keep the tears at bay as she shaved my head. Ems kept squeezing my hand as the razor kept pushing tufts of my hair onto the ground. I looked over at her, and she was staring at me, tears in her own eyes. Mine slipped down my face as the hairdresser worked deftly around my head, and eventually she released the cape, revealing my newly shaved head. It felt cold, and my neck felt the breeze as the door of the salon opened. I had to have cancer going into autumn, didn't I?

The hairdresser brushed off my shoulders, took my scarf, and, with a swirl of material, wrapped it around my head. The scarf covered my lack of femininity. Not having hair horrified me more than I thought it would. The loss stripped away everything that made me feel like a woman.

I worked hard at work, putting in long hours to get everything ahead of schedule. I needed the business to survive me not being there. I was going to turn up every day, but I needed to make sure that processes were in place in case I couldn't be there. I wrote lists of things that Iona needed to know, tried to budget for future productions. Paperwork mounted up as I wrote procedures for everything—how to access the online banking, how to check off inventory. I stopped short of giving Iona approval to pay invoices.

I wanted to know what was going on and when. It got down to the wire. I was up all night the day before my first chemo treatment. And even then, I didn't sleep well.

The first week of June arrived. I wasn't sure what to expect on my first day of chemo, so Iona came with me, plus I wasn't sure I could drive afterwards. All I knew was that I would meet my nurse, Sara Harris. Turns out Sara was amazing. She talked me through everything, what to expect and when to take the pills, because there were pills for everything. And if I took them on time, then the side effects would be minimal. I wouldn't be tough and work out what I could cope with and what I couldn't, so I opted to take them when I needed to. There were pills for nausea, to stop vomiting, and various other outcomes. They told me after I'd shaved my head that the treatment might not actually make it fall out, but it was a chance that I wasn't willing to take. The treatment would make my hair go funny, even if it didn't fall out. Besides, some lucky woman would have a bird's nest of red hair for a wig.

Iona sat with me as Sara hooked up the IV fluids onto the stand and then fed the needle into my skin where the port-a-cath sat. Then all I had to do was sit back and relax. It was hard to relax when I knew that a poisonous chemical was coursing into my body. But I had to stop that mindset. And I didn't know what to talk to Iona about. And I was sick of people asking me how I was feeling. I always gave the bog-standard answer of 'fine', but it wasn't that simple. Some days I felt well, other times my mind raced with endless possibilities of what could happen and the worst-case scenarios. I knew I shouldn't go there, but it was hard to stop them. Especially when it was only me and Ems at home, *if* she was at home.

Carol's Christmas

Iona sat back with her cup of tea and looked around the room. It was comfortable, a recliner chair for me to sit or lie in. I chose to sit. Posters of pretty scenes and motivational sayings plastered the wall. The view out the window was on a large garden setting with a view of the mountains out to the west. I stared at the mountains, enjoying the peace and tranquillity. A rose garden, full of faded blooms and leaves falling off, was a little too depressing to look at. You'd think the gardeners could have come and deadheaded the bushes. As I thought that, a bloom fell to the ground in a shower of faded yellow. It felt like my life; falling apart and crashing to halt.

"That view is amazing, isn't it?" Iona interrupted my solitude. Her gaze was distant, out to the horizon, not focused on the faded roses.

"Yes, they are pretty spectacular."

"What are you thinking?"

"Not a lot, just wondering what life will be like in five years' time."

"What do you see?"

"The business ticking over, Ems at university." I sighed. "Me at home on my own."

"The business will always be there." Iona rolled her eyes.

I laughed. "As long as I'm at the helm, it will."

"That business will run fine without you."

"Will it?" I bit my bottom lip. It worried me not being in control of my business.

"You have no faith in your staff, or me, do you?" Iona looked offended.

"I do, but I want to keep my fingers on the pulse, know what's happening and what's going on."

"Your staff are hard-working. You need to give them more credit than you do. They won't be slacking off because you're not there."

Iona's words needled me. "Of course they're hard-working, but I still needed to have that control over my business. I need that money to keep things going, to pay the bills, to ensure that Ems and I are secure, that she has everything she needs."

"You will always have control over your business, but you might find that you can't be so hands-on soon enough. Let's just take each day as it comes."

I nodded. Because I knew that as soon as we finished here, we would go back to work.

Chapter Sixteen

July

Four weeks into chemotherapy, and I was exhausted. I tried to keep active, but the more active I was, the more tired I felt. This week was a week off chemo, which was nice.

I went into the office for the first couple of weeks after chemo, but by midafternoon, I was ready for a nap.

I'd go home and lie on the couch, intending to just put my feet up for a couple of minutes, and then wake up when Ems came home from school.

"Are you alright, Mum?" she'd ask.

"I'm fine, just tired." I'd get up then and start making tea while Ems went to her room and started on her homework.

Tonight was different. I lay on the couch and fell asleep. But I woke up to the smell of something cooking. I looked at my watch and saw it was six in the evening. And I had a blanket over me. I sat up.

"You looked so peaceful sleeping that I let you sleep," Ems said, sitting down opposite me on the chair.

"Oh, sorry," I said, stretching and yawning. Even though I'd slept, I still felt a deep-seated tiredness.

"Don't be sorry. I've started dinner."

"I can smell it. Smells good."

"I thought I'd make spaghetti bolognaise."

"If it tastes half as good as it smells, it will be fantastic." I grinned at her, and Ems gave me a smile back. It was something, I had to admit, that I hadn't seen on her much lately. My illness was really affecting her.

"How's school going?" I asked. Her smile fell and she kind of sunk down into the seat at the same time.

"It's okay. Coming up to mock exams, so I'm nervous."

"But you know what's happening, don't you? You think you've studied enough?"

"If I do any more study, my brain will implode!" she said.

"You feeling confident?"

"Not really."

"Why not?"

"I get nervous around exams, and I read things wrong."

I smiled at her. "Take things slowly. Don't try to be the first one out. Get in there, take a deep breath and read the questions, all of them, slowly. Then start back at the beginning and read the first question again, and start from there."

"Is that what you did?" she asked, looking hopeful.

I couldn't help but laugh, because it wasn't what I did. "I wish I had. Just take your time. You're a very smart girl. You'll know the right answers to put in there."

"I hope so," she said, putting her hands on her knees and then pushing herself up from the chair. "I have to check on tea."

I heard pot lids rattle as she checked things in the kitchen. I set the table for us and then got a couple of glasses of water.

"No wine tonight, Mum?" she asked.

"No, don't feel like drinking. This chemo is making me feel yuck."

Her face fell. "So, you don't want tea, then?"

"Oh yes, I do. It smells amazing. I'm not missing out on that!"

The look that crossed her face was priceless. She was used to cooking for me, but for some reason, tonight, she was nervous. When the plate turned up on the table, it looked like a professional chef had prepared it.

"Wow, you did this?"

"Yes." She sat down with her plate and picked up her cutlery. I took my time, looking at the spaghetti and how she'd made it look like a nest with the thick tomato sauce and mince sitting in the middle with some parmesan cheese sprinkled on top. A thin watery tomato liquid was oozing out from under the pasta. The smell made my mouth water.

"This looks…" I couldn't keep the pride out of my voice. Instead, I picked up my fork and started twirling spaghetti onto it before plunging it into the mince. I scooped up a generous amount and put it in my mouth.

The flavours…oh, I could wax lyrical about the flavours. They were intense, and amazing and with subtle tones of basil, the beef and the red wine she must have used for the sauce. I closed my eyes, and I felt myself transported to an Italian restaurant.

"This is just fabulous. What is the recipe?" It sure beat my dowdy flavoured bolognaise.

"It's a Jamie Oliver one that Dad has."

"Your dad taught you this?"

"Yip, and others."

I didn't want to talk anymore. I needed more of that delicious-tasting food in my mouth. By the time I got to the fifth mouthful, I was full. I know it wasn't much, but I had heaped the forkfuls up.

"That was the best meal I've had in a long time," I said as I wiped the sauce from my lips on a paper towel.

Ems positively glowed under my praise. How had I not noticed that before?

"Thanks," she said, her cheeks glowing.

"I'm sorry I didn't eat it all, but I'll keep this for tomorrow."

"That's fine," she said, looking a little deflated.

"My stomach isn't handling the medication well. I don't like to overeat or I want to be sick, and after that amazing meal, I don't want to be put off it," I offered as a way of explanation. Ems nodded.

I took my plate and covered it with plastic wrap, and put it in the fridge. That would be my lunch tomorrow.

I started doing the dishes, rinsing and putting the smaller stuff in the dishwasher, but I noticed that there wasn't much. Apparently, my daughter had been cleaning as she was cooking.

How had I not noticed her becoming a young lady? She was growing up, and I was still treating her like a ten-year-old. Instead, she was capable of making a wonderful meal and cleaning up after herself.

She brought her plate in, rinsed it, and put it in the dishwasher.

"You off to study?" I asked. It was normally what she did after dinner, head off to her room.

"I'm not feeling in the mood to study. I might just listen to some music."

"Would you like to play a game of cards? Snap? Last card?"

"They're kids' games, Mum."

"What about Euchre?"

"I don't know how to play that."

"It's simple enough. I can show you."

I got the cards out, and we set ourselves up at the dining room table. I gave her a brief rundown of how to play, and then we did a couple of open-handed games before Ems decided she knew what she was doing.

"Okay then, let's do this."

She played her first card, a trump card.

"Well, that's not fair," I said, pulling out the only card I had in that suit. She grinned as she pulled the cards towards her. She laid out her next card, the other bow card. I rolled my eyes and played an off suit. At this stage, her grin was looking pure evil. What had I done to my child? She won the next two cards, but I got her with the fifth, stopping her march.

"You picked that up way too fast for a beginner," I said narrowing my eyes at her.

"Beginner's luck," she announced, looking proud of herself.

"Beginner's luck, my arse," I said.

She beat me at the game.

Chapter Seventeen

July

Iona decided we needed a work party, so organised a midwinter Christmas dinner to motivate everyone. I made it to the office most days, but I finish early because of tiredness. At least I'm sleeping well at nights.

Tonight, we're heading to the Italian Place for the Christmas dinner. I don't know why Italian, when we could have had a good Christmas meal at some other restaurant, but I didn't plan it, so I kept my mouth shut. Ems is coming with me, and everyone is going to be there with their partners. I didn't really feel like going, and I've warned about low immunity because of the chemo could lead to a cold or flu, which would mean I'd have to delay treatment. But Iona insisted and even bought me a fancy mask I could wear.

The door opened and Ems walked in to the lounge. She looked terrible. "You okay?" I ask.

"No, I feel really grotty. I don't think I'll go with you tonight."

"Okay," I said, resisting the urge to hug my daughter. She's sick, and my natural reaction is to comfort her, but I can't. "I'll stay home too."

"No, you won't. You're going," she said as she dropped her bag on the floor of the kitchen. She grabbed a glass of water before continuing. "I've rung Dad, he's taking you."

"But I don't want him to take me."

"Too late," Ems grumbled. She shuffled off to her room, minus her bag. My heart rate increased, and I felt a sweat break out on my forehead. Maybe I'm sick too. I picked up my phone and rang Noah.

"I'll pick you up at six," he said, instead of hello.

"I'm not feeling well," I said, a hand still resting on my forehead. My heart raced as I spoke to him.

"I'm coming around."

"No, don't. I can't afford to get sick. Ems is sick,"

"Then I'll look after both of you," he stated.

"No!"

"Either way, I'm coming around, so you're ready or in bed," he said.

My mouth went dry and squeaked out a response. "Bye." I hung up.

My heart rate settled down, and I wondered what that was all about. I wasn't feeling sweaty now either, instead butterflies were circling my stomach. I looked at the clock. It was nearly four.

Damn, did I want to go with Noah? Hell yeah, except he was my ex-husband. I mean, we've separated; we haven't finalised the separation or anything yet, but I still loved him. I wanted to have a tantrum in the lounge, but realised that wasn't really the best way to get organised. Instead, I rushed into my bedroom and rummaged through the wardrobe, discarding clothing items until I realised I had nothing to wear. Nothing would fit. It was too big and baggy. And no time to buy something else. Instead, I would have to throw together some ensemble. I grabbed a rather long skirt and pared it with a black lacy long-sleeved blouse. It looked sufficiently party like, without being over the top. My hair was no longer stubble, but it would feel nicer after a shower.

I think I actually sang in the shower, as I lathered up and scrubbed at my spiky scalp. By the time I'd got out of the shower, my hair was curling slightly, so it looked okay. The tiredness I felt earlier in the day was gone. I dressed, carefully selecting some sexy lingerie, even though I knew Noah wouldn't see it. It was nice to feel sexy for a change. I sprayed some of my favourite perfume on and almost regretted it after having a coughing fit. I grabbed the stool from the kitchen and sat down in front of the bathroom mirror and attempted to put some makeup on. Normally for work, a little mascara and lippie were all I needed, but tonight, I wanted to look special. Instead, I ended up looking rather ghoulish with the black eyeliner, so I removed it and tried again. This time I opted for a blue eyeliner, and gently lined my upper lid. Mascara finished my eyes off. I put some sparkly highlighter on my cheeks and I liked the effect. I put on a subdued lipstick and felt ready to go.

I went through my wardrobe again, looking for a clutch, and slipped my phone and credit card into it. Iona had the company credit card, but I took mine in case I needed a taxi home, because although I was excited about Noah coming to the Christmas do with me, I also knew that at some stage, we would eventually argue, and I would need to get a taxi home.

I sat in the lounge and waited. Butterflies had turned to birds that dipped and dived in my stomach. I hadn't felt like this since Noah and I first met. We weren't high school sweethearts; we met once we'd left school and started working.

There was a knock at the door, and Noah came in. He wore black jeans, a white button-down shirt, and a black suit jacket. My heart fluttered in my chest, and I remembered all over again why I fell in love with him. He always made an effort. And he was handsome. So damned handsome. Even the sparkle in his eye was still there. He came over and kissed my cheek. "I'll just check on Ems, okay?"

I nodded and got up from the chair. Once again, I regretted the decision to go. I just wanted to stay at home with Noah and Ems and make believe that we were a happy family again. I paced around between the kitchen and the lounge, fighting the emotions that were burning under my skin.

"Ems is asleep," Noah said as he came back through. "I didn't go into her room, but she sounds all stuffed up."

"She didn't look great when she came home."

He came over to me with a sweet smile on his face. I had a fluttery feeling in my stomach and my pulse increased as he approached.

"Look at you, rocking your short hair." His hand brushed up the back of my head. It was a sweet gesture, but it was also something I missed about him, raking his fingers through my hair and pulling me in for a kiss. I sighed.

"You okay?"

"I'm tired."

"How's chemo going?"

"It's going."

"Like that, is it?"

"Pretty much." I smiled at him, though I knew it wasn't a sunny smile. "I'd much rather stay home."

"And I've been told to haul you out."

"By who?" I turned to him as he offered me his arm. I linked my hand over his elbow and he led the way outside.

"Ems, Iona."

"Oh," I said. I walked silently beside him as we got to his car and he opened the door for me. I slid into the passenger seat and pulled my billowing skirt in with me. He shut the door and came around to the driver's seat.

"This is almost like old times." He smiled.

"It is." Small talk was awkward. I didn't know what to say.

"How's work?" I asked him.

"Busy, which is good."

"Hmm." Too busy to see me. Was it code for being busy with his girlfriend?

I stayed quiet as he drove the car to the restaurant. He pulled up at the park right outside the door. But my mind was racing in overdrive about Noah and his girlfriend. How had she let him come out tonight with me? That was a question I didn't want to ask.

"Wait here," he said. He got out and ran around to my side of the car and opened the door, offering me his hand to help me out. I took it, and he helped me onto the footpath.

"You look stunning tonight." He smiled as he bent over and kissed my hand. HE KISSED MY HAND! I swooned and I felt unsteady on my feet. He'd never done that before, but that moment made my head go all giddy, and for the first time in ages, I smiled, an actual cheek aching smile.

Chapter Eighteen

July

The back room at the Italian Place was rowdy, and cheers went up as soon as I entered. Iona came over and hugged Noah, then me. "I didn't think you'd come."

"I didn't want to. Noah made me," I replied, but my smile was a happy one.

"He looks good on you," she said, winking at me.

"He's only here because Ems and you made him," I said pointedly.

"I doubt that he would have come because Ems told him to," Iona said, handing me a glass of wine. I looked at it and shook my head. I was tired enough without having a wine. It would probably make me go to sleep.

"Juice will be fine," I said. Iona pulled a face, but asked the barman for an orange juice. Noah had already left my side to talk to the husbands of my employees. He knew most of them, and they'd looked shocked at him coming in on my arm. I guess they're a bit confused, like I was. Why would he agree to bring me tonight?

Iona led me to a table and sat me down. Employees all filtered over, one by one, asking me how I was, if there was anything they could do for me. I shook my head and just told them to work hard. Some looked away awkwardly, others smiled politely and left. Eventually, it was just me and Iona sitting there. Servers brought food out, and people gradually sat down to eat their meal. The atmosphere in the room was lively, everyone excited. After the main course, Secret Santa gifts were handed out. Everyone had picked a name out of a hat of a fellow workmate and they had to buy a gift for them. The opening of gifts prompted many gasps and exclamations, along with a few tears of appreciation.

And it hit me. I wouldn't have known what to get any of my staff. They were my workers, yet I didn't know them as actual people. I was stunned. So much thought went into the gifts purchased and included a Marilyn Monroe picture that was fairly rare. The gift receiver cried as she opened it up and realised what a piece of art it was. I would never have guessed she was a Marilyn Monroe fan.

Another worker got a voucher for books. Apparently, she's a bookworm. I didn't know that. And as the evening drew on, I felt left out of conversations, because I didn't know my people. They got together in groups and talked, moved on, and talked, and I sat there and watched, as no one would come and approach me, except Iona. These were people I'd picked to work with me because of their skills, and yet, I knew nothing about them.

One lady had a sick kid at home. He'd been home for over two weeks, and both parents had used up their sick leave.

Another worker's husband was on disability because of a workplace accident. I knew the accident had happened because she'd taken time off to be with him, but I didn't know that he couldn't return to work.

I wanted to help, but I didn't know how. I could give them cash, but that would be less money in the business account if we needed it. And after the Covid shutdowns, I couldn't donate any money for fear of another shutdown.

"You alright?" Noah asked, coming to sit beside me.

"I'd like to go home now," I said, yawning to emphasise my point.

"You haven't had dessert yet."

"I don't feel like dessert," I stated before taking a deep breath. "Sorry."

"Apology accepted. I'll grab your coat," he said, and walked off.

"I'm heading home," I said to Iona as soon as I found her, giggling with some of the staff.

"Don't go yet," she implored, but I shook my head. I was exhausted. And with all of what I'd witnessed tonight, I was beyond shattered. My mind was a whirlwind of information that was overwhelming me.

"I need to go home and rest." I smiled at her and the team. They smiled back at me and wished me well. "See you all Monday," I said as Noah placed the coat around my shoulders. I kissed Iona's cheek and turned to leave.

I sat quietly on the drive home. So much was going on in my head. So much I had missed while in my business, about people I was supposed to care about, yet I had neglected them all in the name of profit.

"Want to talk about it?" Noah asked as he parked the car.

"Not particularly. Something upset me."

"Did someone say something?" Noah was cute when he was defensive. He was ready to be a superhero and make right any wrongs.

"No, just people."

"Well, we know you aren't a people person," Noah said.

The comment floored me. "I'm not?"

Noah swallowed. I watched his Adam's apple bob in his throat.

"Well, you don't deal with people well. You're a businesswoman. You go after the deals, the sales."

"And?"

He ducked his head.

"Your staff are people, and they make the product. You get what you want."

He was saying it nicely, but I understood what he meant.

"I do?" I hadn't realised I was such a callous, cold-hearted person.

"You treated our marriage like a business too."

"What do you mean?"

Noah turned to me, undoing his seatbelt. He took my right hand. "Honey, you were so focused on making money and products to sell that you didn't have time to focus on us, on our family. You told me and Ems what needed to happen and when. School at eight thirty." He ticked off points off with his fingers. "Me to work by nine, pick up Ems at three p.m., come home, get Ems to do homework...Every moment of our day accounted for, down to the last second. We did everything that you wanted: cooked, cleaned, washed dishes, hung out washing, and did the groceries. With not so much as a thank you, or an 'I appreciate you'. Why do you think Ems and I are so close? It's because we spent so much time together as you were too busy for us." His thumb rubbed over my knuckles.

I closed my eyes. My ears were humming, but I took a deep breath, trying to calm the inner demon that wanted to jump down his throat. I kept taking deep breaths, trying to keep the tears from falling.

"I didn't realise."

"We couldn't tell you. You were too busy to listen."

"I'm sorry," I said, truly feeling the hollowness in my chest as I spoke. The same feeling that had scoured my soul when he left me. The pain in my heart tripled as I breathed out. I reached for the door handle and let myself out of the car.

"Wait," Noah called out.

"No, go home, I'm fine," I said.

He got out and hesitated by the driver's door.

"I'm okay," I said, walking up the path, waving behind me. I didn't want him to see the tears that were trying to fall.

He waited until I unlocked the door and turned the outside light out. I stood hidden behind it and listened as he started up his car and drove away, my heart breaking as it did every time he left the house.

I was such a nasty bitch. How had Iona stood next to me for so long? Was I a bitch to her too? I stripped off my clothing as I walked into my bedroom and left the clothes on a pile by the floor. Looking at myself in the mirror, tears spilled down my cheeks and onto my chest. I looked at my scarred breast, caved in on one side. I looked as ugly on the outside as I felt on the inside. My face was blotchy, my mascara was running down my cheeks like some sadist emo, and my eyes were puffing up. I pulled my comfy pyjamas on and crawled into bed, allowing myself to cry until I fell asleep.

Chapter Nineteen

August

It was coming up to Ems's birthday, and I'd been needling her about what she might want.

We were playing Euchre, a favourite evening game.

"A car?" she suggested while putting down her trump card.

"Not going to happen."

"But everyone else's parents are buying them cars."

"And I bet they don't appreciate them as much as one they would've paid for by themselves."

Ems frowned as she considered what I'd said. I placed my card down, letting her have that trick.

"Dad and I promised you that we'd go halves when you find the right car."

"Yeah, okay," she grumbled. I knew she wouldn't want a cheap two-thousand-dollar car, but something a bit more reliable and low-maintenance.

"Clothes?"

"No, I've got plenty." She placed her next card down after some careful consideration.

"You're turning down clothes?" I reached over and put a hand on her forehead, but she batted it away, grinning at me.

"Music?"

"Spotify, Mum."

"Okay, so what else?" I placed my card down, grinning at her and taking the trick.

"Ugh. I don't know, Mum," she said.

"Well don't complain if I get you a hundred-dollar voucher from Pandora's then."

She rolled her eyes, but I had an idea of something I could get her. She bought me the necklace at Christmas time with our birthstones on it. Maybe I could get something for her charm bracelet.

I was rather proud of myself on the sixteenth of July to produce some small packages for Ems. She looked up at me and back at the two packages I'd handed her.

"At least it's not a gift voucher," she said.

"Then you won't want this," I replied, holding up an envelope. She gave me a funny look before snatching the card out of my hand. She opened it, and a fifty dollar note fell out.

"Fifty bucks, Mum?"

"Open your presents." I couldn't wait to see her expression. She opened the first box, which were noise cancelling earphones. "So, you don't have to listen to me whining about how sick I am," I said. She half-smiled at me.

"Thanks, Mum."

"What? I thought I'd done a good job getting those."

"I prefer earbuds," she said, looking down at the earphones.

"I tried." I shrugged.

"Thanks, I appreciate that." She hugged me, and I could tell from her face that she knew I had done the best I could.

She opened the next box and pulled out the three matching charms, each had our birthstones on it.

"One for you, one for me, and one for your dad," I said, because I knew she didn't have those charms. I'd already checked.

"Thanks, they're cute."

"I know it's Pandora, but I also knew you didn't have those ones."

"You did good, Mum." She kissed my cheek and leaned into me, admiring the three stones: amethyst, aquamarine and ruby.

"Why do you think I kept asking you what you wanted?"

"You should know, Mum."

"Hey, I'm working on it."

"I appreciate that. You up for dinner tonight?"

I pulled a face. Fresh fruit and vegetables were about all I could stomach at the moment. "I'm not up to going out, but you go with your dad."

"I was thinking of cooking dinner here, for the three of us."

I closed my mouth. As much as I wanted to see Noah, I didn't want him to see what an emotional wreck I'd become.

"Go out with your dad, then you don't have to cook."

"But I want both of my parents with me." She pulled the puppy dog eyes on me. She was so lucky that I was a sucker for those eyes.

I sighed. "I'd love to help you..."

"No, Mum. You rest. Dad can help out if I need it."

"Okay." My heart was heavy at my own tiredness and not being able to help Ems, especially on her special day. The fact she was making her own birthday dinner really scoured out the hollowness inside.

"Go, Mum. Rest." She shooed me out of the kitchen and started preparing the meal.

Nerves skittered and my belly fluttered at the thought of Noah coming around. My hair was a patchy mess, and I probably had dark circles around my eyes. Best I went and had a nap before Noah arrived.

After a delicious dinner of roast chicken and vegetables, followed by apple crumble, Ems got out Sequence, a board game we'd recently purchased. We showed Noah how to play, then spent an hour laughing and joking with each other.

I noticed Noah sit back and watch me and Ems, playing, laughing and talking.

"Well, this wasn't something I expected to see," he said.

"What?" I asked, wondering what he meant.

"You, playing games, laughing and talking."

"There's been little else to do in the evenings, and Ems and I started doing this. It's been fun, hasn't it Ems?"

"I've learnt so much about Mum, and look, she actually tried for my birthday." She lifted up her wrist with her bracelet, showing him the three birthstone charms.

"You got one for all of us?" he asked, grinning at me after inspecting the charms.

"You are her father."

"I thought you said the milkman was," Ems said, quick as a flash. Noah's jaw dropped as he looked between the two of us laughing at him.

"You told her that?" he said, laughing.

"I had to explain why she didn't get your beautiful eyes."

"What?" He leaned in closer to look at Ems's eyes, making her giggle and close them.

"Hers are exactly the same as mine," he said.

"I know!" Ems and I were still laughing at him as he shook his head.

"You two," he tutted. "I don't know." He continued to shake his head as he sat back and crossed his arms. He was grinning, so I knew he wasn't offended.

"Right, young lady, I know you're seventeen now, but it's now your bedtime." I announced. Ems pulled a face at me, but came over and gave me a hug and a kiss before giving Noah one too.

"I'll be there in a minute," he said.

"Night," she called out to me.

I went to get up, but Noah reached across the table and rested his hand on my arm. Heat rushed through my blood, and I felt my cheeks flame.

"How are you doing?"

"I'm...okay."

"Are you?" He leaned in, his aftershave wafted with him.

"A little bit tired, that's it."

"You didn't eat much, tonight."

"When have I ever eaten a lot?" I asked. Noah nodded, but his stare kept boring into me. I glanced away, tears threatening to fill my eyes.

"I'm coping, okay?"

"Hey," he said. I turned to look at him, but it hurt so much. I wanted him, with me, helping me, reassuring me that everything was going to be alright. But instead, he had a girlfriend.

"I'm here if you need me," he said.

"Iona and the staff have been helping me out. It's all good."

I had to get him out of here, before I became a huge emotional mess all over the place. My bed was the only place I allowed myself to cry. I needed to be strong in front of Noah.

"You guys are really starting to hit it off, aren't you."

"She's my daughter," I replied, maybe a little too tightly.

"I meant, games evenings, having a laugh. It's the happiest I've seen her in ages."

"As I said, not much else to do when I don't have work to do."

"You're coping very well," he said, finally removing his hand. "I better...go and say..."

"Yes, goodnight."

"Night, Carol." He kissed my cheek and left the room. My cheek felt like it had been seared by the hottest rock on earth. I wished it was more than a chaste kiss that he gave me, but it was all I was entitled to.

Chapter Twenty

August

As winter ground on, returning to work after each chemo session was harder to do. I was feeling sick, though not vomiting, and because of that, I was barely eating, and I was constantly tired. I only had chemo once a week, but it took a day or two for the effects to hit me. And they hit me hard.

My morning routine was to get up and exercise first thing in the morning. I'd rug up against the cold, wearing a pair of tights with jeans, a singlet, merino long sleeve top, a cotton long-sleeved top, and a jersey with a down jacket over everything. A pair of gloves and fingerless mitts kept the frost from my fingers, and two pairs of socks on my feet kept my feet toasty. Two beanies and a scarf kept my head warm. And it wasn't even a cold winter, but I could feel the cold seep into my bones. Regardless, every day I got out and walked around the block.

I was losing weight, too, which made it harder for me to exercise. The lethargy was the worst. I'd get home and just crash on the couch and sleep. Sara kept telling me to eat or at least take the medication she'd prescribed. I did, but I often needed to take them with food, which was hard when I had no appetite.

But I knew when I needed to rest.

I went to work twice a week, and Iona always said the same thing.

"Things are going well."

"Really?" Why didn't I believe her?

"Yes, our orders are going out early, and because of that, we're getting more orders."

"Are they coping?" I meant the staff, and Iona knew. She rolled her eyes at me.

"Yes, they're thriving. In fact, they're working so hard and fast during the day that we've been finishing early on a Friday if we have completed our quota for the week."

"Really?" Now I totally didn't believe what she was saying.

"Yes, and every day, the staff are asking how you're doing, and wanting updates."

"Are they?" Why would they be concerned about me, unless they think I'm going to die and they could lose their jobs?

"Yes, they're worried about you. They want to make sure you're doing alright."

"Even the one whose husband is on disability?"

"Sally, yes. She is the most vocal in asking about you."

My heart ached. Why would someone be concerned about how I'm doing? Their concern was touching. I felt a warmth in my chest as I contemplated my workers' caring thoughts.

"Please tell her I'm okay, and looking forward to getting back to work."

"She will be pleased to hear."

My phone rang one afternoon, startling me from my nap.

"Hello?" I answered, my mouth dry.

"Hello, darling, how are you?"

"Mum, hi, I'm good."

"Are you? Really?"

"Well, as good as can be expected." I stifled a yawn, stretching my arms up one at a time, switching the phone over to the other ear.

"And what is the expected?" she asked.

"Um, I'm halfway through chemo. I'm tired, nauseous, other than that, I'm alive."

"Well, that's good to hear about you being alive. But Emma is worried about you." And there it was.

"Ems worries about everything," I replied.

"No, she doesn't. I find her very level-headed, so her messaging me that she's worried about you makes me concerned."

"There's nothing to worry about, honestly, Mum. I'm fine."

"Maybe I should come down."

I sighed. "Mum, there's nothing here for you to do."

"I could cook and clean."

"Ems and I are managing."

"I could…"

"Look, Mum. I appreciate that you want to come down and make sure I'm alright, but we're fine, and I'm not really up to much. I have Iona and Noah to help out if I need anything." I pinched between my eyes as I closed them.

"So, you don't need me."

"Don't be like that, Mum." I dropped my head into my hand, wondering how this conversation had deteriorated into a guilt trip already.

"Be like what? I offered to come down and help, but you're not interested, so that's fine. I'm pleased you're feeling okay." She ended the call before I could respond. I put my phone down and shook my head.

I loved my mum, but I knew that she would be here a few days, and we would start arguing. It wasn't what I needed right now, and she didn't either. But I couldn't explain that to her. I know that she was a hard worker and got us through the worst of our poverty, but once I started earning my own money, she started charging me board. I was only twelve and had a paper run, when such a thing existed. I had to pay Mum ten dollars a week, which was most of the money I earned.

Dad was working by then, too, so it wasn't like we were tight, money-wise. It turns out she was putting the money away into a savings account, so when I finished college, she handed me the details. She could've at least told me what she was doing. Instead, I resented her for taking so much of my hard-earned money.

Even with the bank account, I tried to keep it going, but living in student accommodation, the costs were high. I still use that original bank account for my savings. There's a little nest egg in there for a rainy day.

It dawned on me. When was it considered a rainy day? That money could sit in there forever, and I'd never use it. Perhaps now was the time. If ever it was raining, it was now.

In the evenings, Ems and I played games and catching up with our days, although I mostly lived vicariously through her because I wasn't up to much. She told me how her day was at school, something funny that might have happened, or some teacher who'd exploded in class because of something another student did.

"How did you get on at school, Mum?" she asked me one evening. I guess I hadn't talked much about my childhood, so she didn't know what my life had been like. I didn't want her to have the same struggles I did.

"I did alright at school, enough to pass and go to university."

"I know that, Mum. What was your favourite subject?"

"Oh, that's easy, history."

"Really?" Ems cocked her head to the side as she contemplated my answer. "Never thought you'd be a history buff."

"I was. I knew everything there was to know about the French Revolution, the American Revolution, and the affairs of Europe before World War Two."

"Wow. Why were you so interested in those things?"

"I guess it was because much could be learnt from the conflicts and the results. How one side wanted one thing, and the other side was normally resistant to change. But it had to change for the rights of everyone."

She looked at me, one eyebrow raised—so like her father. "So why do you insist on being such a bitch to everyone? Why do you resist change?"

Words failed me. First, my seventeen-year-old daughter seldom swore in front of me, and second, because she was right. I focused on rolling the dice and moving my counter around the board, trying to think of what the answer was, but I was struggling. I looked up at her; she was still wanting an answer.

"I guess I'm just worried that we won't have enough money."

Ems sat back. "But, Mum, look at this place. Look around you, we have the best appliances, the best house on the best street, Dad was earning good money, I'm at a wonderful school, and yet, you're worried we'll run out of money?"

I sighed. I guess she was old enough to understand now.

"When I was younger, Dad struggled to find a job. Mum worked crappy jobs, trying to make enough money for us to have food on the table. Dad barely ever worked. Sometimes we didn't have enough food to last us until the end of the week when Mum got paid again. We wore hand-me-down clothes that were patched to within an inch of their lives. When I was about ten, Dad finally got a good-paying job he could stick at, and our lives changed, but I was determined to never be that poor again."

I looked up at Ems and saw this look in her eyes. A strange look. She got up, came around the table and sat next to me, putting her arms around me.

"We'll never be like that, Mum. There's enough food in the freezer to feed a small army."

I laughed, because she was right. We had plenty of meat and frozen vegetables to last us at least six months. "You're right, darling."

"Plus, I can always find a job to help you out. You don't have to work so hard. I've really enjoyed having these evenings together, playing games and talking.

I nodded, sniffing back the tears. I was enjoying the games too. Where once upon a time, I would have been in my office after dinner, planning, marketing, making new prototypes. Instead, I felt more relaxed, peaceful even, and I felt closer to Ems, for the first time in ages.

"Thank you," I told her, pulling her in for a side hug and kissing the top of her head. Her hair was all prickly, and I could see where she'd been scratching her scalp.

"Had a phone call from Nanna, today," I said, lifting my head to look at her.

"Oh?"

"Yeah, she said you were worried about me."

"I am worried about you. You don't look well, you don't eat much, you look like you're about to die, Mum."

"It's just the treatment, Ems. As soon as the chemo is finished, I should start to look and feel better."

"You're not going to die?"

"Not anytime soon." I smiled at her. She snuggled back into my shoulder.

"I love you," I murmured into her head.

"I love you, too."

Chapter Twenty-One

August

Iona came around early, just as I was heading out for my walk around the block on a frosty September morning. I had five weeks of chemo to go. I'd been marking it off on the calendar, anticipating when I'd have no more treatment.

We weren't so much walking as wandering, because I didn't have the energy to go very far. I tried eating; I tried medication; I wrapped up warm; I tried acupuncture; I tried everything, but I had to let the chemotherapy take its course.

"Work is going well, before you ask," Iona said. I smiled at her as I continued to plod. "And I'm sure you've seen the bank statements."

"Yes, I have. The money is coming in. How are you managing that?"

"I ring them up and politely remind them they have some of our product, and if they want it all, they'd better pay up."

"And that works?"

"I guess it's all in the tone," Iona said, looking at me. She'd heard me growling at most of our creditors, and I thought it funny that her way worked better than mine. I guess threatening people with debt collectors probably isn't the best way to get money from them.

"Thank you," I said. I turned to look at her, truly look at her. Iona and I had been friends since college. We were in most of the same classes together, but whereas I was more focused on business studies and accounting and economics, Iona had followed her passion for sewing and cooking.

"Why have you stuck with me?" I asked her.

"What do you mean?"

"Why are you my friend?"

"I could always see through that tough bullshit exterior of yours."

I barked out a laugh, because she always called me on my faults. "Yes, you could. You're the only one who knows how tough I had it as a kid."

"You realise that we're not at school anymore, that we're adults and earning a great wage?"

"Yeah, had that pointed out to me the other night by Ems."

"She's a clever girl."

"I know."

"I guess I knew you wouldn't have many friends in the world, and you always tolerated me, so I stuck by you."

"Tolerated you? Man, you are so easy-going compared to me. I'm wound up like a spring waiting for it to release and break."

"I know, and I'm here to pick that spring up, straighten it out as best I can before coiling it all back up again."

"You've done that so many times for me."

"I know."

We laughed, because it was awkward, and we both knew it. We continued in silence until we got back home. Over coffee and biscuits, I asked how Sally from work was.

"She's fine. She's been asking after you," Iona replied.

"Tell her I've had better days."

"I'll let her know. In fact, why don't you tell her yourself?"

"I don't have the energy for work," I replied.

"Let her take you to chemo one day."

"But I wouldn't have anything to say to her."

"At least you could get to know her."

I bit the inside of my mouth. Perhaps I could. "Okay," I said.

The following week, Sally picked me up from home.

"Morning, boss," she greeted me at the door.

I smiled as I snuggled a scarf around my head and neck. "Call me Carol." I insisted.

"Okay, boss." She winked at me. I couldn't help but smile back as I shut the door behind me.

I got into her little car, and we headed off. I directed her to the treatment centre.

"Come in and have a coffee while I have my chemo. More fun than sitting in a cold car."

"Okay. Thanks." Her smile was genuine and warm.

I sat in the big chair and introduced Sally to Sara, my nurse. Sara hooked me up and asked Sally how she had her coffee.

"Can I have a tea, please?" she asked. Sara nodded and headed off.

"How is it going?" Sally asked me.

"Rough. I struggle, but only four more to go."

"It's tough, I know."

"How do you know?" I asked her, although I winced at the question sounding so harsh.

"I had cancer, leukaemia when I was younger."

My eyes bulged at her. "Really? Wow, I would never have thought you would've been through something like that."

"I don't tell people, and only my friends and husband know. But I understand what it's like to struggle."

"I bet you do. How old were you?"

"I was a teenager. I lost all my hair. It used to be straight and long, but now it's curly, and brittle. Something I have to live with. That's why I keep it short."

"I love your hair. I love the curl in it."

Sally reached up and touched her own hair. "Took a while for it to grow back."

"I'm curious to know what mine will grow back like."

"It's different for everyone. I coped okay with chemo, except for the vomiting. Everything I ate came back up again. I had to have a feeding tube to bypass the oesophagus."

"Oh man, you had it worse than me."

"No, there's always someone out there who is worse off than you. That's how I look at things. I'm alive. Some cancer people I was friends with died."

"That must have been hard."

"It was, but I know they aren't in pain anymore."

"How did you get to be so casual about it? I'm in the middle and I can't see past the end of the day."

"Empathy. You learn to listen and care about other people. Plus, time. I didn't feel that way at the time. I was a bit like you; I couldn't get past the day I was in."

The back of my eyes burned. Here was someone showing me just what she was capable of because she'd been through so much herself. My core echoed as I felt the pain of that emptiness once more.

"How's your husband?" I asked, trying to change the subject before I cried.

Sally sighed. The first time I saw something was wrong. "He's okay, just frustrated. He's capable of work, but not what he was doing."

"What did he do?"

"He's... he was an engineer, but heavy stuff."

"Oh, so he knows how to fix things?'

"Yeah, he's pretty clever at it."

"And nothing else is coming up for him? Work-wise I mean?"

"No, and his case manager wants him to retrain and get an office job. But he's not that way inclined. He wants to work with his hands."

"Like engineering, but on a lighter scale."

"Yes," Sally said, sighing again. "It's hard to see him so frustrated, and while we're talking, it frustrates me. He seems to close off when he's had enough."

"That's hard," I said.

"It's only love keeping us together at the moment."

The news shocked me. "Keep talking to each other, and keep loving each other, and you'll get through."

Sally's smile was sad. "I'll try."

We whiled away the rest of the time with nothing more than chitchat. After I finished and Sara unhooked me, Sally helped me into the car and fastened my seatbelt. I'd never felt so vulnerable as I did then. When we got home, she helped me out of the car and into the house, escorting me to the couch where I had made myself a bed.

"Anything you want? A glass of water? Some crackers?" Sally asked.

I waved her away. "No, I'm good. Thank you for taking me, Sally. I really appreciate it."

"No worries, boss. Take it easy."

"I certainly will."

She'd given me so much to think about. How had I become less of a human and not understood that my staff were actually people, and not only that, but some of them would understand what I was going through. I just didn't know which ones would.

Chapter Twenty-Two

August

The following week, Bianca, a sweet girl, came to pick me up. I almost didn't hear her knocking on the door; I happened to be standing there and heard it. As I opened it, she stepped back in surprise. Her hands fluttered to her chest.

"Oh, hi. I'm Bianca," she said, then her face flushed. "But you already know who I am." She looked down then back up at me. "I'm here to take you to…ah…to your chemo?" she stuttered.

"Hi, Bianca, yes, I know who you are. How are you?"

"I'm good thanks…ah…Ms Sawyer."

"Carol is fine." I smiled at her, and she attempted a smile back, but her nerves probably wouldn't let her.

"Okay, Carol." Her face flushed again.

"I'll just get my things," I said, grabbing my handbag from the hall table where I'd left it. Taking my keys from the hook by the door, I stepped out and locked the door. I turned, nearly bowling over Bianca who was right behind me. I'd expected her to have headed for the car.

"Oh, sorry," I muttered.

"Sorry, Ms…I mean, Carol, I wasn't sure if you needed a hand to get to the car." Her words tumbled out as she tried to explain herself. I smiled politely and indicated that I'd walked out of the house without assistance.

"Oh." She ducked her head, her face glowing so red, I could almost feel the heat.

"Bianca?" I said, getting her attention.

"Yes?"

"I'm okay to walk on my own. I get tired afterwards, but I can still get around. And will you please just relax."

"Sorry, I've never been around anyone with…cancer before," she said as we walked to the car.

"How old are you?"

"Nineteen."

"And you don't know anyone who's had cancer? Then you are one of the lucky few that haven't."

We got into the car, and she managed to get us out onto the road and heading in the right direction.

"What's it like? You know, to have cancer? Oh, that's rude of me. You don't have to answer that if you don't want to."

"No, it's fine. I didn't know I had it until I felt a lump in my breast. It wasn't like I was sick or anything, I just had something that didn't feel right."

"And they removed it?"

"Yes, and most of the breast with it."

"Do you feel unbalanced?" She asked with such innocence. I sat back, because I hadn't really thought about that, but she was right. For a couple of days, I kept leaning more to the left than normal.

"Yes, but I got used to it fairly quickly." I smiled at her, and she shyly smiled back. It was surprising how much it transformed her face, which was clear of makeup, except a little mascara on her lashes.

We got to the clinic, and I invited her in.

"Me?" she asked, pointing at herself.

"Beats sitting in the car," I said.

"Okay."

"You'll get a hot drink and a biscuit. Sara will make sure of that," I said, opening the door to the lounge. I walked in, greeting my fellow patients.

Lucinda was there with her husband. Both waved to me. Matt sat with his earphones on, his blanket tucked up around his chin. He rarely interacted with anyone else, just turned up on his bicycle, had his treatment, and then cycled off again.

Beryl smiled and nodded but kept talking on her phone. The only person I didn't see was Seamus, but it could have been his week off.

"Hello, Carol, and you have a new friend with you today."

"Hello, Sara, this is Bianca, she works for me. Bianca, this is Sara."

Bianca smiled and gave a quick wave as she hid behind me. I sat down in the large La-Z-Boy and wrapped the blanket around my legs. I was already rugged up for the cold morning outside, but sitting for a period of time, I knew I'd get cold. I took of my jacket, and undid the buttons on my blouse, allowing Sara access to my port-a-cath. Sara took the bag from the tray she'd been carrying and placed in on the pole beside me. She traced the line from the bag and placed the end into the port-a-cath on my left-hand side.

"A wee bit of a cold flush," she warned. She said it every time, and every time the sensation of cold liquid flooding underneath my warm skin felt weird.

"Coffee with milk?" Sara asked me.

"Can I have a glass of water today, please?"

"Going off coffee?"

"Yeah," I nodded.

"Told you, didn't I," Sara wagged her finger at me, grinning like an idiot. "That's okay. And, Bianca, what can I get you? Tea? Coffee? Hot chocolate?"

"Coffee, please."

"And how do you have it?"

"White with two sugars."

"You need sweetening up, do you?" Her laugh was infectious. She leaned over and rested a hand on Bianca's shoulder. "I'm just teasing you."

"Oh, sorry," Bianca said.

Sara was still chuckling as she headed off.

"Sit down." I indicated to the lounger next to my chair. It wasn't a La-Z-Boy, but it would still be more comfortable than standing. She sat but perched on the edge of the seat.

"Sit back, relax, this will take a bit." I said, indicating the bag of fluid hanging above me. She settled herself further back in the chair and crossed her hands in her lap. She looked around the room, taking it all in. The other patients and the quietness of the room. The only noises were the whispered conversation between Lucinda and her husband, and Beryl, who was still talking on the phone.

"How long have you...been coming?" she asked.

"This is week seventeen."

"And how long—more—have you got to go?"

"I have chemo for twenty weeks, then radiation."

"Radiation for twenty weeks." Her voice squeaked.

"No, only two weeks."

"Oh." She looked small and awkward sitting in the chair.

"Tell me, what do you do when you're not working?"

"Um...I-I like to read, play games...and I-I..." Her cheeks flushed again. "I like watching old movies." Her hands started fidgeting in her lap, and she looked down at them.

"What's your favourite old movie?" I asked, expecting her to name a John Hughes movie from the eighties.

"*Gentlemen Prefer Blondes*," she replied.

"Marilyn Monroe and Rita Hayworth," I said.

"You know it?" Her face lit up with interest.

"Yes, I've watched it a couple of times. My favourite Marilyn movie is *Some Like it Hot*."

"With Jack Lemmon," she smiled, seeming pleased she'd remembered one of the actor's names.

"That's the one."

"I also liked *Citizen Kane*."

"Oh, I found that too heavy for me,"

"You did? You didn't find it fascinating that he was such a shallow person that really didn't care about anyone but himself?" she asked.

"That's why I didn't like it. He was so self-centred and didn't really care about anyone else."

"Yeah, that's because he didn't want to leave his parents. He had the idyllic life, and they sent him away. That was why he said Rosebud when he died, because that was the name on his sled."

"Still doesn't mean he couldn't have been nicer to people."

"True, yes."

We sat in silence before Sara bustled in with another tray, this one held a mug, a glass and a plate of biscuits.

"Thought I'd give you a variety of sweeteners." Sara winked at Bianca before heading off to check on someone else.

"I've had some ideas," Bianca said quietly. "For work."

"What sort of ideas?"

"About things we can do. To make more money." Her face was glowing again, but I was curious. It'd taken her a lot of courage to talk to me about something she thought I might be interested in.

She proceeded to talk out her plans for what we could do, and they sounded really good. We had the machinery and equipment there; it wouldn't cost a lot more in materials to produce.

"That sounds doable. Have you spoken to Iona about this?"

"No, I haven't."

"Why not?"

"Because I didn't think that it was my place to tell her what to do."

"But you're telling me."

That made her look down at her hands again. I reached over and put my hand over hers.

"Bianca, they're great ideas. I think you should talk to Iona."

"Really? But aren't you the decision maker?"

"Yes, I am, but Iona is in charge at the moment."

"I...um...thank you," she said, lifting her head up and blessing me with a beautiful smile.

Chapter Twenty-Three

August

Liz took me on my second-to-last chemo treatment. Liz was the newest member of the crew who worked for me and still had so much enthusiasm. It frightened me a little how much she had, but I listened to her suggestions.

"And I think if we tweak the machines a bit here, we could make them run a lot smoother, and therefore more efficient. We just need a light engineer to come in and service the machines weekly. Those machines would really hum. It's a real bummer when one goes down. I mean, we have the spare machines, but you have to make sure it's running right before you use it, and if we just had someone who could do running repairs and make sure the spare machines are all set ready to go, then we wouldn't have any downtime at all."

She stopped for a breath, and I held my hand up. "Breathe," I told her quietly. She turned and looked at me, and smiled, a beautiful smile that lit up her face. I smiled back because it was so infectious.

"Are we having trouble with the machines again?"

"Not a lot, but it was just a thought."

"It's a great thought, and I think I know the person who could do that."

"Do what? The machining?"

"Yes, Sally's husband."

"Oh yes, he'd be great." Her eyes lit up. "He'd have the knowledge and the ability because our machines are just smaller versions of the ones he used."

"How do you know?"

"Because I worked with him at his previous job. How do you think I knew about this job? Through Sally."

"Are you an engineer?"

"No, I know the basics, enough to get me into trouble," she said, giggling.

"I know what you mean. I had to teach myself how to run the machines at the beginning, but now I have you guys, I don't have to."

"I love my job. These machines are so much more precise and easier to handle. And the end product looks so much better, and the quality is superb."

"That's because I have staff who know what they're doing," I said, nudging her, and causing her to have a fit of giggles again.

She chattered all the way home, and when she left, my ears were buzzing and ringing so hard. But she had a good point and was very knowledgeable about the machines.

I took a breath once I got inside and closed my eyes. Another deep breath and I pushed off the door and headed into my home office. I sat down in the chair and picked up my phone, dialling Iona.

"Hey, how are you doing?"

"All talked out."

"Liz?"

"Liz."

I heard Iona laughing down the phone. "She's a firecracker, that one."

"But she has some great ideas."

"She does."

"So, I need Sally's home phone number."

"What for?"

"I have a proposition for her husband."

"A proposition?" Iona sounded suspicious.

I laughed. "Don't panic. He's an engineer, he used to work with machines like ours. I thought that getting him in to work might help with downtime, and we wouldn't have to send the machines away to get repaired."

Iona loved the idea. "Do you want me to ring him?"

"No, I'm good," I said as I leaned on the desk and put my head in my spare hand. I was tired, but this was too good an opportunity to miss out on.

"I'll talk to you later, okay?" I said.

"Take it easy," Iona said.

"I always do," I replied, smiling as I imagined my friend's worried face.

I took a deep breath, because I needed to get the noise out of my head. I was tired, and I really wanted a rest, but I had to do this first.

The phone rang twice before a gruff voice answered the phone. "Phillip speaking."

"Hi, Phillip, it's Carol Sawyer here, Sally's boss."

"Has something happened to Sally?" His voice was tense.

"No, not at all. Sorry, I didn't mean to upset you. I'm actually ringing to offer you a job."

"What? You know I can't work, right? I can't do office work."

"But you know how to handle machinery, and according to Liz, you'd be fantastic at fixing our machines, which are just baby versions of the ones you worked on previously."

There was a pause and a scratchy sound, like he was rubbing his hand over his face.

"I don't know what to say."

"How about you pop in and see Iona? She's going to show you around and talk to you about what you can and can't do."

"I can go now."

I laughed at his enthusiasm. I'd been like that once. "Head on over whenever you want. She knows you're coming."

"Wow, thank you, Carol. I really...thank you."

"Thank me once you think you're ready for the job," I said.

"Okay, I'll owe you," he said.

"No, you won't," I replied. "Bye, Phillip," I said and hung up.

My brain was buzzing again, but this time it wasn't from anxiety or tiredness. In fact, I didn't feel tired. I felt warm, and the empty pit inside me seemed to somehow not feel as hollow as it had.

Instead of sitting on the couch, I got up. I smiled and hummed as I moved around the kitchen and got myself a snack. It was coming into spring and the sun was shining, so I took my sandwich and drink outside to sit on the recliner on the patio. I lay back, closed my eyes, and allowed the sunshine to warm up my body. After a few minutes, I peeled my scarf off from around my head and neck. A soft breeze wafted around with the smell of jasmine in the air. It wasn't a cool breeze, but it raised goosebumps on my neck. I shivered but settled back down on the recliner. I listened to the birds in the trees around our property, the sound of the traffic farther off in the distance. I took a bite of my sandwich and chewed slowly, enjoying the flavours of the salmon and the lettuce in the fresh bread. I swallowed it and had a drink of water, which was cool and so refreshing. I sighed as I allowed myself to fully rest for the first time in ages. All the while, the fuzzy feeling of doing something right kept me smiling and happy thoughts danced through my mind as I slowly drifted off to sleep.

Chapter Twenty-Four

August

While it could have been a celebration, my last chemo session wasn't. I was tired, and so over my weekly trip. Noah picked me up, his usual chatty self, while I remained quiet. Not that I didn't like him talking, I didn't mind him filling in the silence. But I was tired, mentally and physically.

I got into the centre and sat down in the chair, waiting for Sara.

"Hook me up," I said, trying to smile at her, but failing. Tears were close to the surface. Noah held my hand, his warmth infusing me. I closed my eyes and sat back, familiar now with the cold fluid that flowed into my body.

"What's up?" Noah asked. "It's your last treatment. You should be celebrating."

"I would if I could." I looked at him, and he studied me. The smiled dropped, and he reached for my face with his left hand, his right still connected to mine. He cupped my face, and I leaned into it, allowing the tears to fall.

"Hey, it's okay." He swiped away the tear and moved to sit on the arm of the chair, pulling me into his chest. Oh, how I loved his chest. I loved cuddling in it, smelling his masculine sandalwood scent. I cried, just letting all the tears flow. I had tried to stay strong for so long and only allowed myself to cry at night in bed because it was safe for me to cry there. No one could see me, no one heard me, no one could tell me to stop crying. My safe space. But this last treatment...it felt strange, but I just let it all out. I didn't try to stop it. I needed a release. The last twenty weeks had been hard. Full of appointments, tiredness, nausea. I'd needed all my energy to get through. But now I'd run out.

Between Iona and my workers running me to my appointments, I'd been doing things on my own. Ems, bless her, had been making dinner, but she was too young for me to lean on. I'd enjoyed the games evenings we'd been having, but I'd had to face the emotional side all on my own. I'd had to put on the happy smile when people turned up at the door. I'd had to talk when I didn't feel like talking. I'd learnt a lot about my staff, but they didn't know half of what I was feeling going through this cancer journey. Ems was just a teenager, trying to cope with school and a sick mum. She didn't need me to put emotional pressure on her.

Iona had been good, but again, she was running the business and had her own family. I guess I felt sorry for myself. I stopped crying, but stayed cradled in Noah's arms, enjoying a respite from the harshness of what my body had been through.

"I'm tired," I said.

"I can see. You been sleeping okay?"

"When I get to sleep, yeah."

"Who's helping you?"

"I'm helping myself. Everyone else is busy."

"Come on, Carol, don't be a martyr."

"I'm not. Ems is cooking dinner, but she can't be a crutch for me. And Iona is busy with work and has her own family. I'm just coping on my own."

"Oh, honey, why didn't you say anything?"

"Why would I say anything? You've got your own life going on. You have a girlfriend."

He jerked away, looking down at me with a frown marring his handsome face. "A girlfriend? Who told you that?"

We both spoke at the same time. "Ems."

He smiled at me. "I don't, have a girlfriend, I mean. She's just a friend, we haven't been...you know."

"What, sleeping together? Why on earth not?"

"Because it's not that kind of friendship. We just catch up once a week for a meal and a chat. I'm mentoring her as she grows her business. Nothing more than that."

"You're a handsome man. Why haven't you pursued anything with her?"

"I'm not interested."

"Why not?"

His face flushed as I looked up at him. He pulled me closer so I couldn't see him.

"I'm just not. Besides, I still have you to think of."

"Why would you think of me? We aren't married anymore."

"Well, technically we still are." He squeezed me. "Until we sign divorce papers, we're still married."

"Okay," I said, feeling that pull in my gut where my emptiness sat. Mention of the *D* word made me shudder. It wasn't something I wanted, but perhaps Noah did.

"So why didn't you ask me for help?" he said interrupting my thoughts.

"You're busy and got your own life, and besides, I didn't think you'd come and help me."

"I took you to your midwinter Christmas work dinner, didn't I?"

"Yes, but that was because Ems asked you."

"Carol, I'm still here for you. Always. I love you."

I pulled away from him. "You still love me?"

"Of course." His face was glowing red now, and I couldn't help but smile.

"Why? I pushed you away for so long. Why would you still love me?"

"You were my first love. We had Ems together. Love changes as we matured. Love isn't always about sex. It's about being together and spending time together. I miss that. I miss you."

"You'll make me cry again," I said, snuggling into his chest.

"Would you like me to help you? Your radiation is coming up. That won't be nice."

"No. Would you? Please, would you stay and help me?"

Noah bent down and kissed the top of my head. "I will."

I smiled as I felt the small thrill of peace wash through my body. That and the familiar pangs of sexual urgency. Something I hadn't felt since Christmas time.

When we got home, Noah took over. He put me in bed and told me to nap for a while. It was nice to give control over to someone else for a change.

I woke up about an hour later and wandered into the kitchen. Noah had made a sandwich for me, and a cup of tea. I didn't tell him I'd gone off tea and thanked him anyway. I ate in silence, enjoying the taste of the sandwich. The tea washed it down, and then he suggested we go for a walk. I wasn't feeling up to it but thought that perhaps it would be good to get out of the house. I'd been pretty much housebound since halfway through chemo, and the only visits out had been to the therapy rooms. I rugged up warm and we headed out.

The sunshine was lovely, and signs of spring were showing with fresh green shoots, various blossoms coming out. Bees buzzed in the air and the breeze was warm. We shuffled our way around the block, and by the time we got home, I felt more aware and awake than I had in ages. I hadn't realised just how much the chemo had taken out of me, or perhaps it was my attitude. I'd been trying to do everything on my own, and it was tiring.

Having Noah in the house was like a breath of fresh air. Ems was thrilled when she got home and found her dad there. Even more thrilled when he said he was staying for a few days. Heat rushed to my face as my chest tightened, because I wasn't sure where he was staying. With me in our room? Was it too much to ask him to stay? As much as I wanted him back in my bed, I knew that wasn't where he would be sleeping. I tidied the spare room; it was already tidy, but unused and closed since winter. It made little sense to heat that room if it wasn't being used. The surfaces were slightly dusty, so I got a cloth out and started wiping down surfaces, being careful not to swirl the dust into the air. No one liked to come into a room and sneeze. Looking at the sheets, I thought the bed could do with fresh sheets. There's nothing like crawling into a bed with crisp new sheets. I stripped the bed.

"What are you doing?" a voice boomed behind me. My hand shot up to my chest to stop my heart from pounding out of it.

"Changing the sheets," I said, turning to look at Noah, who had his hands on his hips and trying to look stern.

"I'm perfectly capable of doing that."

"I know, but I was trying to help," I said, sitting on the bed and puffing.

Noah sat down beside me. "You okay?"

"Just puffed. It's my new normal. I'm fine."

"Let me help you," he said, and I smiled.

"Okay."

He headed to the linen cupboard and brought fresh sheets. We had the bed made in no time. It was nice to have the help and to realise that it was okay to ask for help. I wasn't totally useless, but I couldn't do it all myself, not at the moment, anyway.

When we finished, I collapsed onto the bed, and Noah flopped down beside me, his arm falling across my stomach.

I turned my head to look at him. He was smiling at me. "Like old times," he said.

I smiled and rolled onto my side beside him. "It is a little, except you never slept in the spare bed."

"No, I didn't." His smile slipped a little, and I saw the hurt in his eyes. Hurt that I had created.

"I'm sorry. For being a shit wife."

"Hey, it takes two to make a marriage work."

"That wasn't what you were saying weeks ago," I said.

"Yeah, well, it does. I could have worked harder to make you see what you were doing or sucked it up and worked harder at making it work."

"And I wouldn't have listened or even noticed. In fact, I didn't notice. I didn't actually know until you packed your bags and told me you were leaving, and I still didn't believe it when you walked away. I guess I was waiting for you to come back."

"I wasn't planning on coming back."

A pain pierced through my chest, and a lump formed in my throat. Time slowed, but I felt tears stinging my eyes.

"Thank you for coming to help me," I said, knowing that after I was back on my feet, Noah would probably leave again, and maybe this time for good.

Chapter Twenty-Five

September

Two weeks after chemo finished, I had a visit with Rebecca.

"Everything looks good, let's get this out of your chest," she said, pointing to my port-a-cath. I looked at her, then back at that part of my chest.

"What? Here? Now?"

She laughed. "No, it's a small procedure, but you'll be under general anaesthetic."

I breathed out, relief flooding through my body. "Phew, for a moment there, I thought you were going to whip out a scalpel and cut it out here and now."

"No, it can have scar tissue holding it in there, so we prefer a more humane way of removing it."

"Okay." I relaxed a little and allowed myself to smile.

"How are you doing?" she asked.

"Honestly, I'm doing okay. I've been struggling to eat, but I did beforehand anyway." I held up my hand. "And I have been taking the anti-nausea pills."

Rebecca nodded as she listened.

"I'm finding a new lease on life that I didn't realise I was missing. I'd been so focused on work, I'd forgotten what it was like to rest and be with my family."

"Everyone has their own revelations about life with their own journey with cancer. You just have to remember that life is what you make of it. And to take it one day at a time."

"I wasn't focused on that, though. I was too busy looking into the future, trying to predict what would be needed for jobs and finding ways of making more money. But people are more precious than money."

"Sounds like you're healing nicely." She smiled, and it took me a moment to realise that she wasn't talking about the physical healing.

The surgery to have the port-a-cath removed was short and sweet. Rebecca asked me if I wanted to keep it, but I said no. I didn't want anything to remind me of my battle with cancer.

The next day I sneaked into work early to catch up with Iona. I didn't want to see anyone else because I was tired and wasn't looking that healthy.

I walked quickly through to the office.

Iona opened the door before I could reach the handle.

"Hey, how are you?" she asked, pulling me into a big hug. I squeezed her back, so thankful for her friendship.

"Tired," I replied.

"You look tired."

"Thanks, I need to sit down."

"What are you doing here?" she asked.

"It was too quiet at home."

"But you need to rest."

"Who said I was here to work?" I asked, sitting down in my cold leather chair. The chill made me shiver as I pulled my scarf up to cover my mouth. We had a heater in the office, but it wasn't very efficient. Iona, bless her, noticing my shivering offered to pull the heater around for me.

"You know what? How about we get a heat pump put in here."

"What? That's unnecessary, isn't it?"

"You want to freeze in here every winter?"

"Well, no, but..."

"And cook in the summer?"

"No."

"So, why don't we do that."

"What? Put in a heat pump? Are you sure?"

I understood her confusion; I'd refused her request for years. "Yes, this office is either a sauna or a freezer. Let's do something about that."

"Okay," Iona said looking at me sideways.

"I'll get onto it now," I said, turning on my computer.

Iona sat down at her desk, staring at me, her mouth open. "Are you sure?"

"I know you've been at me about doing this for a while. I thought it's about time I dealt with it."

"Uh...*ooo*kay," she dragged out the vowel as she spoke.

She sat and watched as I went through searches then arranged for a couple of retailers to provide a quote.

I got off the phone to the second guy and looked at her.

"All sorted. AirAway will be here tomorrow at ten thirty and Plumb-In-Air will be here Thursday at nine. You okay with that?"

"Yes? And you want them to send the quotes to you?"

"No, you decide. Get them to install ASAP."

Iona slapped her hands down on her desk, making me start. "Who are you and what have you done with my friend, Carol?" she demanded, grinning at me.

"Let's just say, Carol is having a midlife crisis."

"Well, don't let it go to your head."

"What if it already has?"

"Then, let's hope it's a long-lasting habit."

I laughed at her. "I think it will be. I've learnt some hard lessons these last couple of months."

She crossed her arms as she studied me. "Like what?"

"That I worked too hard and left little time for much else, like my family, and my staff."

"Family are more important."

"But staff are my second family. Did you know that Sally had cancer when she was young?"

"No, I didn't."

"Yeah, so she understands exactly what I'm going through."

"Makes sense now why she kept asking after you."

"And Bianca and Liz, they have some great ideas."

"Yes, they do."

"But I wouldn't have taken any notice of them or their ideas a few months ago."

"You're right, you wouldn't have."

"I just wish that it hadn't taken having cancer to make me see the error of my ways."

"Perhaps it was the wake-up call you needed."

I nodded. "Maybe. Anyway, just got to get through the radiation, then it's full steam ahead."

"I hope you don't mean coming back into the business like there is no tomorrow."

"No, I plan on things being a little different."

"Like?"

"I don't know, but things will be different." I smiled at her.

"What are you planning."

"Nothing. I'm working on some things, that's all I'll say right now."

"Okaaay." She dragged out the word like she didn't believe a thing I was telling her.

"You'll see."

Chapter Twenty-Six

September

Three weeks later, with a fuzzy head of hair, I went in to the office. It was lunchtime, and I'd called in at a bakery on my way there. I arrived to much fanfare with my offerings and everyone clamoured to talk to me.

Phil was the first to greet me. He jumped to his feet and embraced me in an enormous bear hug. After he put me down, he thanked me profusely, and Sally was next. They looked at each other and smiled, and I saw the happiness and love of a long-term relationship right there in that moment, and I felt like an intruder.

Liz nearly bowled me over in her enthusiasm to welcome me back. While Bianca hung back and waited until everyone had come and talked to me before greeting me with a shy smile and a quick wave. I walked over to her and gave her a big hug, making her blush.

I ordered the machines off and led the way into the kitchen for an early lunch with the offerings I had. We all sat and I told everyone of my progress, then we broke off into little groups to catch up. It felt a lot different from the midwinter Christmas party, where I was excluded. This time, everyone wanted to talk to me. Me! The one that used to treat them like workhorses.

After lunch, I met with Iona in the office. She had all the paperwork out for me to check over and reported that everything was going fine.

"Enjoying our nice warm office?" she asked.

Catherine Mede

I looked around and saw the heat pump unit on the wall above the door and noticed the temperature in the office was so much nicer.

"Bet it makes a difference."

"I set it to come on an hour before I come in and turn it off every night when I leave. It's bloody amazing. Thank you."

"No worries. How is Phil fitting in?"

"He's amazing," she said, stretching her arms wide. "We've had no major stoppages since he started. It's been wonderful. What made you think of him?"

"It was Sally and Liz, actually. Liz used to work with Phil, and Sally told me he'd had an accident at work and couldn't go back there. These machines were smaller than the ones he worked on, so it seemed a natural fit for him to work here."

"He is truly the best thing that has happened here for a while. We are ahead of our usual productivity and have enough stockpiled for Christmas and any extra orders that pop up over the holiday period."

"That's fantastic. Well done," I said, turning to smile at her.

Iona glowed and ducked her head. "They're working to make things easier for you."

"Bah," I said, waving away her comment.

"They are. They want to make sure the business is here for you when you come back. They want the company to keep working, even when you're not here."

"Really? I didn't think they cared that much about me."

"They care more than you think. Especially after Sally, Liz and Bianca took you to your treatments. They came back talking about you. You managed to encourage them all, and that's reflected in their conversations with the others."

"Hmm," I said, nodding as I thought about my workers. They'd really stepped up to the mark, something I hadn't expected.

"And how are you?" I asked her.

She took a deep breath and let it go. "I'm doing okay."

"And your family?"

She narrowed her eyes. "They're all good. Why?"

"Aren't I allowed to ask my friend how she is? How her family are?"

"Well, yes, but that isn't like you."

"It is now. You've always been there for me, made me meals, taken me to appointments, and ran this place while I haven't been here."

"I'm just doing what anybody does for a friend."

"No, Iona, you've really gone above and beyond for me. And I can't thank you enough. I really have been a shitty person, haven't I." I lowered my head. My chest was heavy again, and I felt fatigue pulling at me, and the ever-present buzzing in my ears.

"I'm sorry I put so many expectations on you. You've been a veritable saint while I've worked everyone to the bone."

"Hey, I'm just the buffer between you and them."

"You shouldn't have had to be a buffer. I should've been nicer to my staff and my best friend."

"Hey, I know how much you put into this business, how much you relied on it."

"But I lost Noah because of it. How close was I to losing you too?" I asked.

She wouldn't look me in the eye.

"Oh, wow, it must have been close." My shoulders slumped. I got up and walked over to Iona and hugged her tight.

"Thank you for being such an amazing person," I said, as I held her. I could feel her shaking in my arms, and I knew she was crying.

"You can be a bitch sometimes."

I snorted, and I held her close. "I'm so sorry," I said. I pulled away, holding her shoulders and making her look at me.

"I'm realising what a total dick I've been, so please accept my apology. I'm really working on it."

"I know you are, and you've had such a battle."

"Hey, cancer is nothing to losing a friend, and I don't want to lose you. I have lost so much already." I smiled sadly and sat back down.

"Come on, Noah will come back."

"He's made it pretty clear he isn't. He's only helping now because he made me ask. I miss him."

"Then tell him."

"It's a bit late for that, isn't it?"

"It's never too late. You just apologised to me. One could consider it long overdue."

"I have apologised to him."

"There's a difference between apologising and telling him how much you miss him."

"No, there isn't. He doesn't need to know how much I miss him. He's moving on with his life. I don't want to muck it up by begging for him to come back, only to have him leave me again."

"And you know this because...?" Iona shrugged her shoulders.

Mine slumped. I didn't know, but I also didn't want to ask him. When he left, he made it plain that he wasn't coming back. "I guess we'll always have our friendship."

"But is friendship enough for you?"

"It will have to be."

Iona raised her eyes at me, but I couldn't hold her gaze. I didn't want friendship; I wanted my husband back. I wanted the love of my life in my bed again.

"I'll work on it," I said, wondering how I could do any more than I already was.

Christmas Future

"I will honour Christmas in my heart, and try to keep it all the year. I will live in the Past, Present and the Future. The Spirits of all Three shall strive within me. I will not shut out the lessons that they teach!"
Ebeneezer Scrooge

A Christmas Carol
Charles Dickens

Chapter Twenty-Seven

October

Physically, I was tired, but I was feeling better. In fact, it was the best I'd felt in weeks. But the next part was the radiation, and I wasn't looking forward to it. That would be every day. Fortunately, I'd only be there for about quarter of an hour. But it was more poison being poured into my body. And I didn't have Sara there to help me through this process.

It would be more clinical and procedural. I'd already been in, where they lay me down on a bed and placed a massive machine over the top of me. I had to stay still for the minute it would take for the area to be irradiated. Once they had everything sorted, they'd tattooed faint dots on my breast in the precise area they wanted the radiation to go. I would have a reminder forever of my brush with cancer.

A minute was a long time when you're in the machine. The beep that told you the treatment was done was a blessing. And that was only a practice.

I was making the most of each and every day while I had them, because I wasn't sure how my body would cope with the radiation. That was due to start and then it would be two weeks of intensive treatment. Two weeks of Noah being with me every day. Two weeks to talk to him, and convince him to give us another try. I wanted him back. He'd been with us for the last three weeks, on and off, and between him and Ems, the house was looking better than ever. It was nice to know that I really didn't have to do everything.

And I realized, I really don't have to do everything at work either.

Iona was handling things there, and as a result, they already had enough product stockpiled for Christmas. When I worked full time, and the other hours at home, I had to ensure the house was tidy, floors vacuumed, shelves dusted, washing was done. Ems did some, but I did some as well. I hadn't noticed just how much Noah had done around the house until he left.

"You ready?" Noah asked, standing at the door. I wasn't sure I was, but I needed to get through this part. Once this was done, I was over the worst of it. Today was the first day of radiation. This was shorter, so only twenty minutes, but it would be the hardest my body would be affected. I ran a hand over my fuzzy hair. It was coming back more strawberry blonde than ginger, like it had been. It was soft and wispy, like baby's hair, and there was the possibility I could lose it again.

"As I'll ever be," I said, walking up to him and standing at the door, I slowly reached out to open it, while mentally going through a checklist in my mind. I had my cell phone and earphones, so I could listen to an audio book while I waited for my treatment.

An arm slinked around my waist, and I opened my eyes as Noah pulled me in for a side hug.

"You're doing so well. I'm proud of you."

"Perhaps keep the pride until I'm finished," I said, although secretly pleased I was within his arms and allowed myself a deep breath through my nose to take in his masculine scent, along with citrus and hints of sandalwood.

"Did you just sniff me?" he asked.

I smiled at him and ducked my head down. "Maybe?" I couldn't resist. He always smelt so good.

He laughed as he led me down to the car. He opened the passenger door for me and I got in.

We were silent in the car on the way to the radiation centre. It was just around the corner from the chemo rooms. The radio filled the silence with its quiet chatter, but my mind was busy. Having had four weeks off from chemotherapy, I was finding my strength returning, and I was able to do more things that I hadn't done for a while. I hadn't returned to work full time yet, but after chatting with Iona, I knew the business was in expert hands. The business was making money, and from the figures I saw, we were well ahead on last year, so I wasn't worried about that.

I was worried about Ems, though. Ems was studying hard, but she'd spent a lot of time at home with me on my worst days. Even when Noah was there. I couldn't stop her, as I didn't have the strength for the argument, and Noah didn't tell her off either. From what I could understand from her, she was still achieving at school, and as she constantly told me, if worst comes to worst, she could re-sit this year at school. I hope it didn't come to that, but the pandemic had already played up with her schooling, so I guess I couldn't tell her off. I just wish she would attend school like a normal child. I was okay; I had a good prognosis; I knew I'd be okay. I just needed her to see that, too, but being a hormonal teen, I guess nothing really sinks in much. I was thankful that we'd been arguing less. She did as I asked, except go to school.

"What's going on in your head?" Noah finally broke the silence as we pulled up at the radiation clinic.

"Just worrying about things."

"You know you shouldn't."

"Easier said than done."

"The business is running well. You don't need to worry at all."

"It's not that I'm worried about."

"It's not?" He sounded so surprised I looked at him.

"Iona has everything under control. I'm worried about Ems."

"Ems is fine."

"Ems isn't going to school."

"She's achieving her grades, and she is attending classes. She is home on her study breaks."

"That's not what it looks like." I shook my head.

He reached out and cupped my face. I looked up at him. "She's worried about you. She wants to be close to you in case you need her."

"She shouldn't be worried about me."

"And you shouldn't worry either. She's fine. You're fine. Just get yourself better so everyone can stop worrying." He dropped his hand to his lap. I felt the coolness of the air and missed that warmth immediately.

"Are you worried about me?"

"Of course I am."

"I thought you didn't care about me."

"I always care about you."

"Why?"

"Because, despite everything, I love you. That doesn't stop overnight."

"But it does stop," I said.

"Does it? Have you stopped loving me?"

"No, I still love you."

"Then that's all that matters."

"I want you to come home."

"It's not that simple, Carol. I need to see you changing. You're definitely making progress."

I hung my head, feeling the tears stinging my eyes. "When will you come home?"

"I'll know when I see it," he said.

Catherine Mede

With all the things he had done in the last three weeks, running around after me and Ems, getting me to appointments, it was nice to have his company again, but there was still something missing. It was like friends rather than husband and wife. And I missed that so much. I blinked rapidly to get rid of the tears that were threatening to fall, and the hollowness inside expanded ever so slightly again. It had been busy filling up, but I still felt lonely when he was around. I wanted what we had back. Maybe it was too late, it was already gone. It was something I didn't want to face this morning. It was too hard to cope with right now.

"Thank you," I whispered. I don't know if he heard me or not, but it didn't matter. I needed to show him I appreciated what he had done, the time he'd taken off work to make sure that me and Ems were okay.

I got out of the car and headed inside before Noah could follow me. I found a seat and sat quietly. The room wasn't like the chemo room with beautiful views. This was more like a waiting room, with health posters on the wall, a shelving unit full of brochures and old worn vinyl seats that weren't comfortable.

I had barely sat down when they called my name. I had to change into a gown provided for me and put on a cap and mask. I was led into the room with the machine taking up most of the space. It was like a monster with its mouth open, ready to swallow me.

I lay down as directed and listened to the instructions they gave me.

As I entered the machine, my mind went quiet, and again, I entered a moment of mindfulness. I was there, in that moment, as a machine hovered above me, throwing poison at my body. I was there, fighting the cancer along with it. Being at one with who I was.

I didn't have any other choice. I had to breathe in and lie still for as long as I could. Tears could fall, and I wouldn't be able to wipe them away, so I didn't allow myself to cry. Besides, that was for my bed only. For however long it would take.

Chapter Twenty-Eight

October

Two weeks of radiation were hell.

My body didn't cope with it as well as it had with chemotherapy. My fuzzy hair fell out, and I spent a few days crouched over my toilet bowl. All the while, Noah was there rubbing my back and cleaning up the mess afterwards. Not that there was anything in my stomach to come back up, but it was pretty nasty.

After a nap he would get me outside for a small walk around the block, often, with me leaning on him because my body felt so weak.

Ems came home with a cold midway through and had to avoid me for ten days. That was the hardest thing, because she is my life and we both like to have hugs. But because my immunity was so low, we had to keep our distance from each other.

Noah kept me fed up with oranges and lemon honey drinks, plenty of vitamin D, along with plenty of stir-fries with fresh vegetables. It was nice to not have to cook, but often I couldn't eat more than a mouthful or two. He would encourage me to eat more, but I couldn't stomach the food. It wasn't his cooking, it was the fact that I felt nauseous most of the time.

Once radiation stopped, my appetite increased, I felt more energetic. I had to take each day as it came, because some days were good, and some were bad. But each day was progress and I was able to walk a bit farther, eat a bit more.

"You've got a spring in your step," Noah said early one December morning as we walked around the block.

"I'm not leaning on you much anymore either," I said. "I can feel my body recovering."

"That's good," he said, although he didn't sound so convinced.

"It is good." I looked at him. "So, what's up?"

"Nothing," he sighed.

"Don't say nothing and then sigh," I replied.

His smile was sad. "I've enjoyed being around you again."

"I've enjoyed having you help me and Ems."

"I guess...um...I mean...When do you want me to move out?"

His words felt like a shower of cold water over me, and I shook involuntarily.

"When you're ready," I said quietly. We had slowly rebuilt the friendship that we'd had while we were married. And I still loved him. While he wasn't in my bed, I loved having him around. Our conversation from my first day of radiation echoed through my mind, haunting me.

"Okay then," he said, and stopped walking.

"You don't have to move out, you know," I said, taking a deep breath. "It's been nice to have you around, and while we're not married anymore, I do love you and miss you."

"It's been nice to be around. Be with you and Ems again," he said.

"I know you needed some sign, which I don't know if you have seen it or not, but you can stay or leave. That choice is yours, but I would like you to stay," I said honestly. I would be heartbroken if he chose to leave, but I wouldn't blame him. I wasn't the easiest person to live with, and I knew that I had plenty of faults, which is why he left in the first place. And once I got back to work, I wasn't sure if I would return to my old ways or if I'd managed to turn over a new leaf. Iona had done such a great job while I wasn't there, that I didn't even know if I needed to return to work. I wanted to, because I loved working, but would I start pushing boundaries again? How people had stuck by me, I didn't know.

"I think it would be best…" my heart started cracking as he said it. "I think it would be best if I stayed," he said.

I blinked, wondering if I had heard him right. My heart was pounding so loudly I couldn't believe what he'd said. "Pardon?"

"I would like to stay, if that's alright with you."

I smiled before I looked at him from under my eyelashes. "Really?"

"Yeah." He kissed me on the lips, a soft and tender kiss, then took my hand in his. It felt so natural and comfortable and warm. It had been ages since we'd been in public holding hands. In fact, other than at the chemo clinic, I couldn't remember if we'd ever held hands. My chest felt like it was puffing up with pride as I walked down the street, hand in hand with my ex-husband. I knew we were still a long way off repairing our relationship, but this felt like a solid start.

It was another couple of weeks before I went back to work. My hair had started to regrow, the fuzz coming through as a soft as baby hair. It was still red, but somehow it seemed lighter. I liked running my hands through it, because it felt like silk.

When I returned to work, the staff cheered and gave me a standing ovation. My cheeks heated up as I walked to my office. I hadn't expected such a greeting, and my heart swelled and I felt tears sting my eyes. I nodded and smiled and hid myself in my office until Iona arrived a few minutes later.

"You're here," she said.

"I am," I replied, wondering why she was looking at me like I'd grown another head.

"You should be resting."

"It's been six weeks since radiation, I'm feeling rested," I said.

"As long as you feel ready for this."

"Of course, I was born ready."

She smiled, came around my desk and hugged me. It had been a while since I'd seen her, mostly because Noah had been helping out at home, so Iona didn't have to come around. It eased things up for her as she had her own family to take care of too.

"Thank you for everything you did while I was sick," I said to her. I gave her another hug.

"You've already said that, about sixty million times, but you're welcome. It's what friends do."

"I know, but I want you to know how much I appreciate it. You had this place to run around after and your family. I just want you to know that I recognise the work you did."

Iona waved her hand at me. "It was nothing."

"It's something to me," I said as I sat back down at my desk.

"I'll arrange to move my desk out then," she said as she went to go out into the workshop.

"No, I think it should stay there. It would be nice to have the company," I said.

She stopped at the door and stared at me. "Are you sure?"

"This company is still running because of you and those people out there. How could I not have you here with me?"

"Okay, thanks." She left the office and came back about ten minutes later with two coffees. The smell hit me before she plonked it down on my desk. "First things first, meeting with the staff, let them know what we're up to and how things are going," Iona said.

"Sounds good," I said as I got up and followed her out into the workshop. I watched as she conducted the short meeting, with a few cheers and nods from the staff. Everyone looked excited to be there, they looked relaxed and happy. A big difference from the same time last year. When she finished, before everyone went away to work, I drew their attention.

"Ah, I just wanted to thank you all for your help during my illness. I appreciate those who came and helped me and shared stories with me. I just want you to know that I'm sorry for being such a bitch before..." A few awkward twitters of laughter filled the space. "I know that I pushed you guys, but during my time off, you have proven just why I employed you all. You're so fabulous, and I thought you should know that I'm thankful for Iona, and you guys for keeping things going."

There was a smattering of applause before Sally came up and gave me a hug. Phil shook my hand and thanked me again for giving him work. It was nice to actually smile and be friendly with my staff.

Chapter Twenty-Nine

November

The following week, I went back to work for the mornings. I spent time in the workshop, building up rapport with my staff, rather than my customers. I let Iona deal with them; she had developed an efficient system, so I didn't see the need to interfere with that, and she drove some hard bargains. As a result, the company was seeing some great profits coming in.

After years of running the business, it felt great to get back on the shop floor, to spend time with people, and work the machines again. Sally and Phil were an outstanding team. Even though they didn't work together, watching them when they were together was really eye-opening. Watching them openly flirting with each other made me feel all mushy inside. There was something about seeing love being expressed that made me feel that way. It wasn't usually how I did things, but seeing them made me feel that there was a genuine hope for me and Noah. The way they smiled at each other, and I wondered if that was what married life was all about.

I used to take work home and spend evenings working on it. With Iona handling that side of things, I wasn't taking work home. Instead, my evenings were now spent with Ems and Noah. Game nights had become a daily event, with lots of laughs and talking. I'd missed the most important parts of Ems growing up.

The days blurred together as I focused on getting myself healthy again. Noah and I went for walks most evenings now that the sun was out longer with the walk around the block extending to a walk around several blocks.

I'd never felt so healthy and happy.

Noah stayed in the guest room, not once coming through to me in our old bedroom. I missed that, the intimacy.

"Do you miss us?" I asked him.

"Of course I do."

"Why don't you come in and see me at night?"

"Do you want me to?"

"Yes, very much," I said.

"I was waiting for you to ask me."

"Why?"

"Because I needed to know that you wanted me."

"I've always wanted you. I never stopped wanting you."

"You were always too busy with work."

"I know. I was too wrapped up in a misconception that my business wouldn't survive without me." I hung my head, my cheeks heating as I thought of who I'd been. "I'm doing less now."

"I know. And how is that working for you?"

I sat back and actually sighed, a smile pulling on my lips. "Relaxing. It's nice having the evenings to myself. I love our game nights, and our evening walks. It's been fun spending time with you guys."

"That's good to hear."

"So, will you come to bed with me tonight?"

His face flushed, and he lowered his head. He smiled and said, "Maybe?"

I threw the pillow at him and he threw it back, and the next thing I knew we're having a wrestling match on the ground, both of us laughing so hard. I somehow ended up underneath him. Noah pulled back, looked me in the eye, and leaned down, his lips touching mine. The jolt of electricity through my body happened every time he kissed me, and it hadn't changed. Maybe it had intensified, because I wanted to rip his clothes off there and then, but it was daylight and Ems was in the house.

We heard a clearing of a throat at the lounge door, and we looked up to find Ems standing in the doorway. "Now, now, children." She smiled at us and then launched herself on top of us. We were a big family pile of hugs and love, and my heart lifted and felt full for the first time in a long time. We sat up, and Ems looked at us both, her hair tousled.

"Does this mean what I think it means?"

"We're not rushing things," I said, "but"—I turned to look at Noah—"maybe." He hit me with a pillow and I laughed.

Later that night, once Ems had headed to bed, Noah crept into my room. "You awake?" he asked.

"Of course," I said, moving the blankets aside on what used to be his side of the bed. He crawled in, then snuggled up behind me.

"I missed the way you smell," he said, breathing in as his nose buried in my silky, extremely short hair.

I turned over to face him, his arms still encircling me.

"I missed your smell, too, your body wash."

"Mmm, I missed the way you used to snuggle in behind me when you were cold."

"Like this?" I asked, curling up into a ball and tucking in as close to him as I could. He laughed as he smothered me by pulling me in tight against his chest.

"I miss running my fingers through your chest hair." I stroked the soft hairs on his chest. There was something quite soothing in the repetitive action.

"I missed you doing that," he said, lying on his back, allowing me better access.

"I missed the way you snore softly at night."

He snorted. "I don't snore."

"Yes. you do."

"No, I don't." He was grinning at me.

"Okay, then I like the way you breathe really heavily and snort while you sleep."

That made him laugh.

"You snore too."

"I know I do," I replied, happily admitting to it. "I know I snore, and I wouldn't deny that."

We laughed together as Noah pulled me in to snuggle me against him.

"I love the way you sleep. I miss watching you sleep," he said.

"You watched me sleep?"

"Yeah, when we first got together, not so much when you started your business, because you often came to bed after I was asleep."

"Know what I don't miss? Being up half the night trying to get things done."

"I like that too."

His eyes studied my face. "Can I see it?"

A knot tightened in my stomach. Thoughts flitted through my mind, would he or wouldn't he like what he saw. "Yes?"

"If it's too much, I can wait."

"No, it's alright," I said. I rolled onto my back and hesitated. "I'm nervous."

"What of?"

"Your reaction?"

"Why?"

"You might think I'm ugly." The sting of tears prickled behind my eyes. Noah bent down and kissed me.

"You'll never be ugly in my eyes."

A tear trickled down my cheek, my stomach churning, yet there was a piece of hope that uncurled within my chest. I undid the buttons while Noah gazed into my eyes. I pulled the pyjama top open, and without taking his gaze from my face, Noah's hand moved onto my stomach, then gently traced lines up my torso. Slowly, he moved, his touch igniting fires in my nerves as it travelled up towards my broken breast. His fingers explored the skin, sensations tingling in unanticipated areas. He bent down and kissed me, his lips lingering on my lips. I sighed as his fingers explored the area, then my nipple, then his head bent down and he looked at my breast, and without hesitation, his lips followed where his fingers had been. It felt so sensual and seductive, and before I knew it, I was riding on a wave of nervous sensations that built up within me, before I crashed down on the most enormous orgasm I'd ever had.

He looked up, grinning and kissing my face, and finally my lips as my heart rate caught up with the rest of my body.

"I still have the touch," he said, and I couldn't help but giggle.

"Seems you do," I replied, languishing in the after-orgasm glow.

"Roll over," he said, and I was confused for a moment, until he pushed me away and then pulled me back to curl up behind me. I loved it when we spooned.

"Do you not want sex?" I asked.

"No, I want to cuddle you."

We lay side by side, while I was thinking about all the things I'd missed about him. My eyes were getting heavy, and I kissed his arm that was wrapped around my neck, supporting my head.

And I realised. This. This is what had been missing. Being held in his arms like I was the most precious and delicate thing in the world. The real intimacy between him and me.

Chapter Thirty

December

By mid-December, the workshop was humming. Someone had brought in Christmas decorations and tinsel covered the machines and walls, and small slivers decorated the floor. I actually enjoyed the festive season for the first time in years, and seeing everyone happy and enjoying themselves was a real morale boost.

I sat in our air-conditioned office and just relaxed. It was probably the most relaxed I'd ever been at work. I wasn't stressing about the workload or the new orders coming in. We'd produced a surplus during the year, so everything was ticking along nicely.

"You know what?" I said to Iona when she got off the phone.

"What?"

"I'm going to give everyone three weeks paid leave over Christmas and New Year."

Her eyebrows disappeared into her brunette fringe. "You sure?"

"Why? Do we have a big order?"

"No, but last year—"

"Was last year. The team deserves it. Look how hard they've been working. And you especially deserve that time off."

"But *three* weeks paid leave?"

"Why not?"

Iona shook her head. "No arguments from me."

"The accountant said the books look great, which is all thanks to you."

"It was a team effort, Carol. Don't thank me solely."

"I'm not, but I think you're the hardest worker here. You've been the go-between for so many years. I just want to recognise you for what you've done."

"Well, thank you. Do you want me to tell everyone?"

"Nope, I'll do it at morning tea time," I said, smiling.

"Okay," Iona said, though she kept looking at me sideways.

"What?" I asked.

"What have you done with my best friend, Carol?"

I laughed. "Carol has learnt a big life lesson."

"I like this new Carol. She's a lot nicer."

"I like this Carol too. Much more relaxed."

"You definitely needed to relax. Pity it was cancer that made you see that."

My hand automatically went to my soft red hair. It used to be a riot of curls, now it had a gentle wave to it and wasn't as bright as it used to be, but I liked it. It wasn't long, but it was growing, and I was thankful for that.

"Oh, Iona,"

"Yes?"

"I'd like to offer you my job."

"Your job?" Her eyebrows drew down. "What would you do? Retire?"

"No, I'd stay here, but you've proven yourself here, and I'm more than happy to do your job."

"Are you sure?" Her face broke out into a huge grin.

"Of course. You know the job, inside and out. I think we'll create the position of Sales and Marketing Manager, and that will be you."

Iona jumped up and raced around to me, hugging me tightly and bouncing up and down.

"Thank you!" she screamed in my ear. I winced, but couldn't keep the smile off my face.

"You deserve it. And a pay rise as well."

Iona stopped jumping and, holding me at arm's length, stared at me, her mouth dropping open.

"P-pay rise?"

"Of course."

She screamed and started jumping up and down again. I'm sure the staff must've thought I was murdering her. I'd never seen her so excited. She was normally so quiet, even-tempered, but you'd have thought I had made her Mrs New Zealand from her reaction.

"Settle, Petal," I grinned as she let me go and skipped a circle around the office.

She picked up her phone and started calling her husband, John. At least I presumed that was who she was calling. I hadn't told her how much extra she was getting, but she was too excited. So, I used the opportunity to have morning tea and tell the team about the holiday period.

The staffroom was noisy as conversations buzzed around me. I waited until everyone was in before announcing that they had three weeks paid leave over the holiday period, meaning they didn't need to return to work until the start of the third week of January.

A cheer went up, and people crowded around to thank me. Morning tea took longer than normal, but I didn't mind. Everyone was excited, and the atmosphere in the place had a happy vibe. I went back to the office afterwards, and Iona was still on her buzzy high. The entire place felt so different from a year ago, when the staff were in a hurry to have a two-week holiday.

It made me reflect on my year, and how different things were now. How different I was. I almost shuddered when I considered how cold I had been, how focused and driven and single-mindedly I'd focused on the business. And all I could think about was keeping the money coming in. I hadn't trusted my staff or my best friend to manage things, yet they had proven how reliable they were. How I had basically done the complete order for February on my own, to the detriment of my relationships with my family.

I sighed and prepared to do the paperwork that was on my desk.

That night, at home, I told Noah and Ems over dinner what I'd done. Ems smiled, while Noah had a quizzical look on his face.

"Can the company afford it?" he asked.

"Yes, Iona more than deserves it. She hasn't had a pay rise in three years, and the team hasn't had three weeks off since the lockdown. The business has made a good profit this year, so why not share it with everyone?"

Noah's eyebrows rose as he regarded me, then nodded. I wondered what he was thinking, but I wasn't worried about that right now. I was more interested in Ems and how her day went, and then what Noah had been up to.

While Emma did her homework, Noah and I washed up the dinner dishes.

"Are you feeling okay?" he asked me.

"Of course I am. Why?" My insides quivered as I wondered if I was looking pale, or flushed, or if I looked ill.

"It's not like you to offer a pay rise to someone, let alone give your entire workforce three weeks off." He grinned at me, and I swatted at him with the tea towel.

"That's rich. Aren't I allowed to reward my staff?"

"Of course you are. Hey, Carol. I'm proud of you."

"Why?" I genuinely wondered why he was proud of me. He stopped washing the dishes and leaned his hip against the bench as he regarded me.

"You've really turned yourself around. You're not as self-centred as you used to be, and you're showing people how kind and beautiful you are."

I felt my cheeks heat up, and I ducked my head down. "I'm just a lovely person," I said as I leaned against the bench.

He grinned, as he flicked soap suds at me, and I instinctively flicked the tea towel, cracking it loudly against his leg. He flinched, then a spark of humour flashed in his eyes. I squealed, throwing the tea towel at him and ran out of the kitchen, with him hot on my heels. I giggled as I raced around the house, trying to avoid him, but he caught me as I dashed from the couch to the hallway. He picked me up and threw me over his shoulder, taking me down to our bedroom.

I yelped as he dumped me on the bed, then landed on top, nearly winding me. His face was directly above mine, and I grabbed his hair and pulled his lips down to mine. The kiss was everything that it used to be and more. A deep desire uncurled inside of me, and a warmth spread through my body, surrounding me in a lust haze. I couldn't get enough of him, and he was in no hurry to stop. We did, though, both of us breathless. I went to talk, but he smothered my mouth with his. Every time we stopped, and it looked like I'd talk, he'd kiss me, until I was giggling instead of trying to talk. We lay there in each other's arms for several minutes, just being with each other, listening to the other breathing.

It was a moment that I would remember forever, because I now knew, I had my husband back.

Chapter Thirty-One

December

"Carol, lovely to see you," Rebecca said as she shook my hand. "You're looking well."

"I am, thank you," I said as I sat down opposite her desk.

"That's great. Your tests have shown that everything seems to be in order. The cancer has been dealt with, and we'll now move onto the next phase of the treatment."

"There's more?" I asked, feeling a little crestfallen. I'd been through surgery, chemo and radiation. What else was there to do?

"Yes, hormone treatment, for the next five years. This will ensure that everything goes according to plan, and the cancer won't come back."

"Is that guaranteed?" I asked.

"No, it's not. That's why I'll see you next year, and the year after that. We'll take scans and blood tests to ensure that the cancer has gone."

"Oh, okay."

"Carol," the doctor said, trying to get my attention. "It is ninety-nine percent effective. Don't focus on the negative. You've come so far, don't give up now. We've done everything we can, now it's up to you. Keep healthy, eat well, exercise, sleep, take your medication and you'll live a full life and die in your eighties or nineties."

I laughed. "Really? I have that long to live?"

"I'd like to say your hundreds, but that doesn't always happen."

"I'll take until my nineties, then."

The doctor nodded.

"Thank you, Rebecca, for everything. You've made this entire process so much more bearable."

"Thank your friends, Carol. It was them that got you through. I'm just the one that delivers the good and bad news."

I nodded again. She was right. It was my friends that got me through, but her support and treatment got me here today. When I stood up this time, I hugged her. She laughed as she pushed me away.

"You've got a lot more life to live. Go out there and live it."

"I will." I took my script and left, feeling on top of the world.

When I picked up the prescription for the pills, I didn't look at the label or the document with the side effects inside. I was just happy to have a new life. A new start. A new chance to be human and live again. If I focused on what could go wrong, I knew it would put me back into my run-around-like-a-headless-chicken mode, which was basically me before the cancer.

It seemed like a lifetime ago that I sat in Rebecca's office and was told I had cancer. When it was only ten months. In that time, I'd had an operation, chemotherapy and radiation. My hair had fallen out, I'd gotten sick, but it was Iona, Noah, Ems, and my staff that got me through it. They got me up, fed me, took me to appointments, let me nap, run my business, helped me exercise. They were the genuine heroes in my life, and I needed to let them all know how much they meant to me. I'd already rewarded Iona and my staff. I just needed to show Noah and Ems how much they meant to me.

After a detour on the way home, I got there as Noah was dishing up dinner. Afterwards, I dropped my bombshell.

"I've booked us on a holiday to the Gold Coast for three weeks in January."

Ems's eyes opened wide. "Really? Oh wow, how cool."

Noah sat with his glass of wine halfway to his mouth. "Isn't that your busiest period?"

"Yes."

"Don't you want to be at work during that time?"

"Iona has things under control. I don't see any need to interfere."

Noah nodded, before his face broke out into a big grin. "Wow, who are you, and what have you done with Carol?"

"Funny! Iona said the same thing," I laughed. Ems erupted into a chorus of "Holiday" and started dancing around the room before she hugged me as she skipped to the kitchen to start the dishes.

"Well, that is one for the books," Noah said, he got up from his seat, and grabbed my empty plate.

"I wanted to prove to you I've changed and show you both that I love you very much."

Noah bent his head down and kissed me on the lips. Then my nose and forehead. It was gentle, and I knew that we'd finally turned a corner. Those kisses were precious to me. They meant he loved me and wanted to protect me.

"Thank you."

"You're welcome."

"You're certainly heading in the right direction."

"What direction is that?"

"Towards having a husband again."

A part of me thrilled at the words, but another part of me felt chilled by his comment. "You were considering leaving again?" I asked, feeling that heavy emptiness in my chest swallow up the warmth I'd just basked in moments earlier.

"No, that isn't what I meant. Sorry, I meant that…" He put the plates down and knelt beside me and took my hand. "That came out wrong. What I meant to say was, I'm so proud of you. You've been showing Ems and I that we mean something to you. You're managing your work and life balance, and you're letting Iona take over more at work. I see the changes that you've made and I want to acknowledge that. And what I really want to say is…" He let go of my hand and pulled a ring box out of his back pocket. I stopped breathing as my heart soared to the heavens.

"Will you marry me? Again?" he asked. I grabbed his face in my hands and pulled his mouth towards mine, kissing him hard and deep.

"Yes," I said when we surfaced for breath. He laughed as he took my hand and wriggled the ring onto my finger. It was plain compared to my original flashy engagement ring. A gold band held a small aquamarine stone with a diamond chip on either side. Simple, yet somehow it meant more to me than my original engagement ring.

"Yes, yes, yes," I repeated. The hollow core filled up with warmth and love and overflowed out of my eyes as I cried happy tears.

Ems came in at this point. Seeing me crying, her eyebrows drew low over her eyes. "Mum! What is it?"

"We're getting married again." I said.

Ems started screaming and jumping up and down around the both of us as we hugged and celebrated as a family unit once more.

Chapter Thirty-Two

Christmas Eve

On Christmas Eve, the factory shut down at ten thirty. We'd cleaned and oiled the machines, and swept the floor to within an inch of their lives, creating clouds of dust that were whisked away by the light morning breeze. Husbands, wives and partners turned up to have a barbeque lunch cooked by Noah and Phil. Drinks flowed freely, and I'd arranged for taxis for everyone to get home so that everyone could celebrate and be safe if they wanted to.

We had a secret Santa and everyone loved their gifts, especially when I handed everyone a card as they left at the end of the festivities. Sally and Phil ran back to thank me, and hug both me and Iona.

The look on Iona's face as they left was priceless.

"Open yours," I said. Bewilderment pulled at the notch between her eyebrows as she pulled the beautifully printed card out of the envelope. Inside was a lovely note from me, along with a two-hundred-dollar gift certificate, and a card announcing that she had shares in the company.

"You gave everyone one of these?"

"Yes, every one of my employees now has a share in the company."

"Are you sure?"

"How could I not be? This is what I want to do for the people who looked after me when I needed them most."

Tears welled in Iona's eyes, then she hugged me.

"Thank you," she muttered in my ear.

"You're welcome. Most of the staff won't know until tomorrow. It's my gift to them."

The office phone rang, interrupting us. We looked at each other and laughed. "There's always one," Iona said as she swiped at her tears.

"I'll get it," I said, rushing into the office. I could have left it to ring off, but that wasn't a good business practice.

"Hello, Laroc Originals, Carol speaking."

"Hello, Carol?"

"Yes, speaking."

"Hi, it's Amanda here, from Corporate Facilities."

"Hi, Amanda," I said, as Iona entered the office and listened in to the conversation.

"We'd like to place an order for delivery in early February if possible."

"February?" I asked, looking over at Iona. She shook her head, frowning. I smiled and winked at her, as I nodded and said "ah ha" to Amanda on the phone.

"Yes, we'd like to order some of the following...."—and she rattled off the list. I wrote everything down as fast as I could, confirming details with her as I went. Iona was looking at me, no, glaring at me, shaking her head as I wrote things down.

I continued to smile at Iona, sweetly, indicating for her to sit down, but her face looked drawn, and she started pacing.

"Amanda, hang on a minute, I'll hand you over to my sales and marketing manager. She'll be able to help you," I said.

Iona's mouth fell open. I put my hand over the receiver. "It's not my call to make."

Iona looked like she was attempting to talk, but nothing came out.

"It's Amanda from Corporate," I told her and handed her the phone.

"Hi, Amanda, it's Iona."

I didn't listen to the rest of the conversation. I didn't need to. Iona had everything in hand. I went into the staffroom and tidied up, not that there was much to do. The staff had done most of it by the time I'd returned, but a few napkins and glasses were lying on the table, so I washed the last of the dishes.

Iona came into the staffroom and hugged me.

"I seriously thought you were going to take on that order."

"Really? You had such little faith in me?" I replied, stunned by her response.

"Yes, I did. You did it last year, and I thought you'd want to do it again this year."

"I knew you would have it in hand."

"And I do. We have pretty much all the order to ship now, if we wanted to, but it can wait until next year."

"See, I knew you had it all under control."

"Carol, you're a miracle, you know. You used to be such a scrooge, but now…"

"I had a fright this year, and I learned I needed to be a person, and not a machine. In fact, I am only human. I know where I went wrong, I focused on the wrong things."

"You were more worried about money than people."

"Yes, that too. But things have changed now. I won't be back at work until February. I'm taking my family away for a holiday, which might just be a second honeymoon as well."

Iona squealed and leapt up and down. "You and Noah are back together? Oh, wow."

"Yes, and he proposed again," I said, taking the ring out of my pocket where I put it for safekeeping.

Iona studied the ring carefully, turning it over in her hands. "It's small."

"It's perfect. I was too materialistic. This symbolises how I feel now. It's small, because it isn't about the object, it's about what it represents, a pure and simple love."

"Aww," Iona said, tipping her head to one side and her eyes going soft and watery. "That's so romantic." She handed the ring back to me.

Having dried my hands, I put it back on my finger. "I didn't even ask him to propose again. We haven't even divorced, and it wasn't him leaving that woke me up. It was the cancer and having to rely on people. Things can't help me when I needed to get up and moving. The business couldn't drive me when I couldn't. I needed people, but I needed to see past my own insecurities."

"You're insecure?"

I nodded. "My success depended on the business succeeding. I needed the money to make myself feel better. Needed the prestige to feel like I'd accomplished something."

"But you are something. You're a friend, a boss, a wife, a mother," Iona pointed out.

"But I was a shit friend, a snobby boss, a terrible wife, and a worse mother. It's only now that Ems and I are talking like friends. Before that, she would only tell me what I wanted to hear."

"That's her just being a teenager."

"*That* was her trying to cope with an absent mother."

Iona nodded her head.

"I really didn't deserve you, and I'm sorry. I used you so much. But I appreciate everything that you are," I said, pulling her into a hug.

"You have always been an outstanding friend. I could see past the bitchy moments. I knew you were trying to cope with the situation you had. It's okay," she said.

"It wasn't. But thank you for being so understanding."

"You're welcome. Now, go home."

"Yes ma'am." I saluted Iona as I hung up the dishtowel.

"Merry Christmas, Carol," Iona called out.
Merry Christmas, Iona."

Chapter Thirty-Three

There was still one person I needed to talk to and set things right with. I sat in my car, and without overthinking it, I picked up my phone and dialled her number.

"Mum?"

"Hello, dear, what's up?"

"Just ringing to say hello."

"Hello." Her crisp reply told me she hadn't forgiven me for not letting her come down and mother me while I was sick.

"How are you?" I asked.

"I'm good, and you?"

"I'm doing...great."

"Really?" She sounded surprised.

"Yes, in fact, I'm actually ringing to see if you have a current passport."

"Why? Do I need one to get into the South Island?"

I laughed. "No, but you'll need one to come to Australia with us."

"I'm not moving to Australia with you."

"No, Mum," I laughed. "But Noah, Ems and I are going to the Gold Coast for a three-week holiday after Christmas, and we'd love for you to join us."

"You would?"

"Yes, for an entire three weeks."

"Oh, what can I say?"

"Please say yes."

"I'd love to, but I can't afford the flights."

"It's all taken care of."

"But I can't pay you back."

"I don't expect you to. I just want to spend some time with those I love, which includes you, Mum."

"Really?"

"Yes," I laughed.

"Well…I…I'd love to come. My passport doesn't expire for another two years."

"Then we're all good. I'll book the tickets, and we'll meet you in Auckland."

"Okay, what brought this on?" My mother sounded suspicious.

"I want to celebrate life and being with my family. And it was about time that I showed my appreciation to you for everything you did for me when I was growing up. Besides, you remember that savings account you gave me, when I went to varsity? I kept it, as a rainy day account. And while I was sick, I decided that now was as good a time to use it as any."

"What about your business?"

"It's in excellent hands."

"And did you say Noah was coming?"

"Yes, Mum." I screwed up my face, trying not to squeal with excitement in her ear. "We're back together."

"Oh, darling, that's wonderful news."

"Thanks, Mum."

"I knew you two couldn't live without each other."

"Some things needed to change."

"Yes, they did. I'm pleased for you both."

"That's great. Anyway, we're all well here."

"I know. I spoke to Ems earlier."

I smiled, because my daughter was always good at keeping in touch with her grandparents. "So, she told you that Noah and I are back together."

"She's over the moon. And you're getting married again? Ems is happy to have her family back together," Mum said.

"And having you come to Aussie will be the icing on the cake."

A lump formed in my throat, because now was the hardest part.

"I'm sorry for being such a shit daughter."

"Oh, darling...You—"

"No, let me finish, Mum. I was a shit daughter. I always thought you were too hard on me, and I was pleased to get away from you. You made me think that money was everything, and I had to learn that it wasn't. And that it wasn't your fault either. It was because things had been so tight, and I never wanted to experience that again. I threw myself into my business and then turned my back on those who needed me most. Noah, Ems...and you. So, I'm sorry I didn't let you come down when I was sick. I wasn't in the right headspace to deal with everything. Cancer has taught me a few hard lessons, but ones that I don't want to forget, so I wanted to apologise for all the times I was nasty to you, didn't forgive you, and all the times I said horrible things about you behind your back."

There was a pause on the other end of the phone, and I wondered if I had offended her. It wasn't what I'd intended.

"Mum?"

"Yes, darling, I'm here. I'm sorry that you thought money was everything. I struggled every day to make sure that you didn't know how bad it was, but it was pretty bad."

"I knew it was Mum, and I hated watching you struggle, but I didn't know what to do to help."

"There wasn't anything you could do. Your father was the one who should've helped me, not you. When he finally found his feet, that took the pressure off me, but I was so used to doing things that way that I continued to push it onto you. Taking half of your money and putting it into a saving account, I should have discussed that with you first, but I didn't."

"That rainy day account...I realised that if cancer wasn't a wet enough time, what was? So that's why I'm spending it. We don't get to be on this earth forever, and I want to spend every moment with my loved ones, including you."

"Aww, Carol, that's so sweet. I'm sorry too, darling."

"Thanks, Mum. I love you."

"I love you too."

"Well, I guess I better let you go."

"Yes, fabulous, darling, I better pack."

"See you next week," I said.

"Carol?"

"Yes, Mum?"

"Thank you."

"You're welcome."

Chapter Thirty-Four

Christmas Day

It was chaos on Christmas morning in our house. I woke up to Christmas carols blasting from the kitchen. I rolled over and found the other half of my bed empty. Not that I was worried. We'd made love last night. It was passionate, loving, gentle, sweet. It was everything.

I smiled as I stretched, remembering it was Christmas Day.

"Don't get up," said Noah as he pushed his way through the partially closed door with a tray of food. I moved into a sitting position as he placed a tray over my legs, then hopped around to his side of the bed and snatched a piece of toast off the tray. Steaming fresh coffee, toast and a rosebud in a vase decorated the tray. It was so romantic, and so was Noah. I'd forgotten that he used to do these things for me. I leaned over and kissed him before grabbing my coffee and taking a sip.

I could hear Ems at the other end of the house, bustling away at something. "What is she doing?"

"Getting lunch organised."

"She's cooking the chicken?"

"Nope."

"Why not?"

"We got something special planned."

"Oh?" I asked, feeling the smile pull at my lips. My heart felt so full, overflowing with love for these two special people.

"It's a surprise." Noah said, wiggling his eyebrows. Another thing I'd forgotten, and yet I loved it so much.

"Okay." I settled back and finished my breakfast.

After breakfast, we sat down in the lounge to open presents. Parcels were piled up under a small Christmas tree that the three of us had erected on the firebox, decorated within an inch of its tiny life. Noah acted as Santa, issuing out the presents, and we ripped into the paper, throwing it around the room in our haste to check out our gifts.

Noah got me my favourite, Not a Perfume by Juliette Has a Gun. I knew how expensive it was, so I appreciated the sentiment. I got a pair of blow-up breasts from Ems, which was a prank. We all laughed until she produced matching necklaces for her and me. It was two hearts, with Mother and Daughter written on them. Ems had my name on the back of hers, and Ems's name was on the back of mine. It was a beautiful sentiment, which I really loved. I put it on immediately, vowing to myself that I'd never take it off.

I was excited for Ems to open her presents from me this year. I still remember the pain from last year after realising how much I'd failed my daughter.

She opened the first little box to find my original engagement ring. "But this is yours," she said.

"I have a new one. That one is yours now." I'd even had it sized to fit her finger. She looked at me and Noah with surprise.

"Why?"

"Because it's yours. You would've inherited it if anything happened to me, so I thought, why not give it to you now?"

"Thanks, Mum." She hugged me, before putting the ring on her finger and admiring it from a distance.

"Come on, there's more," I said, snuggling into Noah as he sat behind me.

The next present was a large, framed picture, one I'd seen her admiring of a warrior angel. I'd got the print and framed it for her.

"Oh, Mum! Thank you! I've been eyeing this up for ages." She hugged me again.

"You're welcome," I said. She admired the picture before she opened her next parcel. This one contained a diary planner, one that I'd seen online that I knew she also had been admiring. It had been expensive, but it came with stickers, cards, and all sorts of pretty things to decorate it with. I'd even got her the pen and the leather case for it to go into. Her eyes opened wide.

"You knew?"

"Of course I did. You saved it on my phone."

She grinned at me. "So you do look at things on your phone."

"It wasn't half obvious!" I laughed at her.

"Mum, you've outdone yourself."

"No, I've given you what you deserve and wanted. I failed you for so long, Ems. I'm sorry. I love you to bits."

"I love you too, Mum."

I kissed her hair as she burrowed into me for a hug. Noah reached around both of us, and I felt surrounded by love.

"What did you get, Dad?"

"I got you two," he said, smiling.

"Don't be silly. Here," Ems handed him a present. It was a black leather wallet to replace the one that was disintegrating in his pocket.

"Thanks, Ems."

"What did Mum give you?" she asked.

"Your Mum gave me the best gift of all. She gave me you, and she gave me back my family."

"Oh, Dad, she gave you something else, didn't she?"

"Yes, she did," he said. He held up a T-shirt that had 'World's Best Husband' written on it.

"Is that all?" Ems screwed up her nose.

"It isn't about material possessions, Ems. It's about moments and spending time with people you love," he replied, hugging me tight.

It'd been a tough lesson to learn, but at least I got the chance to learn it. I learnt that family is important; they give you support when you need it most. I learnt that best friends really are forever, and will stay with you through thick and thin, even if you don't deserve it.

After breakfast and presents, we got ready, and they took me to the beach for a picnic. I hadn't had a picnic in…I couldn't remember how long. It was nice to have a change of pace. The beach was busy with other Christmas revellers. The sky was a pale blue, and the sea lapped gently at the golden sands. There was a slight onshore breeze which carried the smell of the salt air. I inhaled deeply, enjoying the sun's warmth on my face.

Pleased, once again, that I had this opportunity to enjoy the moment and just be with my family.

Now, I am Carol, wife and mother.

And that is important to me.

If you liked this story, sign up to my newsletter on my website www.catherinemede.com for updates on my books and releases

Behind the Story

2400 women per year are diagnosed with Breast Cancer, in New Zealand.

That's approximately 40 women per week.

It is the most common cancer in NZ women.

600 women die from it each year (about 10 women a week).

85% of women survive breast cancer for 10+ years.

It can be found in men as well as women.

When I was young, Mum had a good friend who had breast cancer, which she ultimately died from. That was over thirty years ago. There's been a lot of research into breast cancer, and now we have a better idea of what causes it, like the BRCA2 gene mutations which can determine family risks of cancer. Nowadays, breast cancer is more treatable, and the mortality rate has decreased by 30 percent over the last thirty years.

I know more women today who have been diagnosed and survived. I spoke to a lot of people about breast cancer, and two very special ladies, Leanne and Trudi in particular were very forthcoming and matter of fact about their cancer journey's. I appreciate the time that it took for them to share their story with me. One thing I learnt from all of the research, everyone's journey is different. Some have chemotherapy, some don't. Some skip radiation, some have all three. Whatever their journey looks like, it is unique to them, and it doesn't take away from the fact that they have faced cancer. They are heroines in my eyes as they have faced uncertainty and came back from that. Often their lives have changed for the better because of it.

So why the story? When I first thought of doing a retelling of *A Christmas Carol*, I knew I needed three 'ghosts' to help tell the story. What made me think of breast cancer, I can't recall, but it seemed like the perfect way to change my protagonist, Carol. She needed to be someone who didn't think much about other people. She is a successful business owner who works hard but expects everyone else to as well. Being diagnosed can be very traumatising, so how would a successful entrepreneur/control freak handle losing control over their body and business? I thought it would be a good way to bring about change within a person to make them understand or accept change.

In *A Christmas Carol*, Ebenezer Scrooge is visited by three ghosts – Christmas Past, Christmas Present and Christmas Future. It is becoming increasingly popular in New Zealand to have a midwinter Christmas, because Christmas for us falls in the middle of summer. So what better way to present the Christmas Past, Present and Future than showing Carol with the three distinct Christmases.

I also wanted to do a second-chance romance, which tied in nicely with the personality of the protagonist. Making Noah, her ex-husband see her changes is what was important to the story because actions speak louder than words. And seeing her changing before his eyes makes him realise that she's genuinely making an effort. Seeing the impact on his daughter is the biggest catalyst. This also helped with the story of Christmas Past and Future. With Carol's Christmas Present being the midwinter, while she is wallowing in her cancer misery.

I've managed to make the story fit within a year, with a little artistic licence. Not everything comes together within a year, and I'd like to acknowledge that everyone's journey takes its own course.

Gratitude and Beatitudes

A very special thank you to those who shared their cancer journey with me, and especially **Trudi** and **Leanne** for their insights.

My writing buddies **Carole** and **Janet** – for their encouragement and support
Serena and **Barbara** for keeping me to my deadlines
LaVerne, my first writing buddy, for editing this story.

To all my fans – (especially **Nicola, Joan, Yvonne, Michelle, Brenda, Estelle, Jeanette** and **Viv**) thank you for buying my books. I really appreciate it.

To those who read my books, thank you for taking the opportunity to check it out. I hope you enjoyed it.

And always –
To my **mum, my son, Sheri and my Mr H** – Thank you for your support and encouragement. It means the world to me that you guys believe in me, even when I'm struggling to believe.

Bobba and Beth – My guardian angels. From the bottom of my heart, thank you for your love and support that I still feel even from heaven.

YOU GUYS ROCK.

Thank you for taking the time to read this book. If you enjoyed it, please leave a review on Goodreads and wherever you purchased this book from.

Who is Catherine Mede?

Catherine Mede lives in Motropolis, in the South Island of New Zealand with her handsome hero, her son and a rescue cat Lunar. When not writing, Catherine likes to read, be crafty and work in her garden.

Although having developed a love for writing when she was at high school, it wasn't until she was in her thirties she decided to really get down and dirty with the words in her head.

Romance and speculative fiction are the genres Catherine likes to dabble in, because hey, why not? And adding fantasy elements fulfils her need to create fanciful worlds.

When she was younger, she wrote to escape reality, now she writes it to allow others to enter a world where love has a happily-ever-after ending.

Stalk Catherine Mede on:

Facebook www.facebook.com/Catherine Mede
Pinterest www.pinterest.com/Catherine Mede
Twitter @Catherinemedenz
Instagram @CatherineMede
Website www.catherinemede.com
Email admin@catherinemede.com